Two Glasses Of Wine

by
Jann England

authorHOUSE®

AuthorHouse™ UK Ltd.
500 Avebury Boulevard
Central Milton Keynes, MK9 2BE
www.authorhouse.co.uk
Phone: 08001974150

First published by AuthorHouse 12/8/2009

ISBN: 978-1-4490-4554-8 (sc)

This book is printed on acid-free paper.

Chapter one

There are times in your life when you wish you could be more intelligent or perhaps more educated in the art of etiquette, yet in real life what people see is the true markings of a professional bimbo. That's me. Full on clumsy, giggling and an unashamed mismatch of dumb, blondeness in its full glory.

I grew up in the eighties an only child in a small town in Lancashire. I came from a good background and even though I had a reasonable education at school, school didn't easily impress me, academically I mean. My parents didn't try to encourage me too much either because from an early age I had decided that my only real ambitions were to be the best personal assistant ever to a top businessman and drive around in a flashy sports car. Theresa Bannister's my name but everyone just calls me Tess, well except my Dad when he wants to impress upon me something of importance.

Even though I went to college nothing really registered with me too much, except fashion. Things never quite work out the way you expect them to. Don't get me wrong I am no duck egg and I am perfectly accepted in the everyday scenario of work ethics. Ultimately I managed to clinch quite a good job within a chain of offices, which enabled me to wear the latest clothes; a small salary like mine could buy.

By the time I had reached my twenties I had a substantial sum of money saved up, compliments of my Dad's good management rather than my good sense. I paid my first down payment on a town centre apartment and furnished it with the bare essentials on a pile of loan agreements. This was to be the beginning of my independence.

A normal day would consist of the usual rituals all women rise to by dragging myself out from under a quilt that looks like its just done ten rounds with a wrestler. Its seven o'clock and I opened the curtains to allow humanity in through the window. As bedrooms go it was quite small but I had quickly stamped my authority on it with a careful choice of white lace bedding and silk and furry cushions, smothering the space on top of my bedroom chair.

With my mouth open wide and the first yawn of the morning, I find myself scuffling off to the kitchen to make my first coffee of the day. I say kitchen, it was an extension to my living room separated by one long workspace of pine cupboards. It tucked itself perfectly into the end of the room, shouldering cupboards either side of it, just like a long corridor. The living room was much bigger and I had managed to fill it with all kinds of nonsensical possessions. Ever since college I have spent some glorious years here and splashed my own mark on the walls in lovely shades of creams and apple white. The living room was by now looking quite cosy and I had established a junk collection to die for. All bought with every good intention to improve my status one day in the worst possible taste. Each corner filled with paintings of all shapes and sizes or books piled to the rafters on subjects I one day will master, but not just now okay. I have to hoard because that's what I am supposed to do. Apparently they become a great talking feature but 'heaven forbid' any one asks me any questions. What do I really know about Harmsworth popular science or Queen Mary of Scots any way? All I do is hand over the book to the interested party and pour the wine, simple.

My first of numerous cups of coffee and I hit the shower. Every woman knows that showers are the opportunity of a lifetime to practice the choruses to a good song, out of hearing range from those that truly love you. In other words, sounding like a strangled alley cat that had just lost the will to live. It was the wakeup call I needed to start me off for the day.

My shoulder length blonde hair gets a ten minute blast from the hairdryer and I'm ready to move on to the more essential things in life. I top up all my new facial lines with cement mix and colour coordinate my eyes and lips with whatever is lying around in my ever exaggerated collection of designer makeup piles that happens to be lying around on the dresser. I quickly check for any telltale smudges to my makeup in the mirror and move on to the wardrobe. I like to collect my thoughts every morning and challenge myself into remembering the wife's name of the next client; I am going to be meeting at 11.00 am, as I spray the bedroom and my clothes with the latest in perfumes that was also taking pride of place on the dresser. By now I am frantically rummaging around the bottom of my wardrobe searching for the appropriate pair of shoes and continue to ambush my collection of designer tops from the drawers with the full force of a disillusioned goat. All my colour coordination techniques eventually pay off when I finally settle for a subtle pastel top and dark, straight leg trousers and cropped jacket.

All I have to do now is tip my head upside down and shake the cobwebs from my hair and straighten my crop into a manageable ponytail, with the latest diamante clasp attached. I rummaged through my jewellery pile and spied the earrings with the multi coloured bundle and started putting them on, whilst still searching for a suitable matching necklace. Draping the necklace down my rather long neck line; I do the last finishing checks in the tall mirror, the one that tells me my bum definitely does not look big in this outfit and I am ready to leave for the office.

Chapter two

The office is not too far from my place so I usually manage to skip across town without too much trouble. It's Friday morning and I can't wait to acknowledge my colleagues with some light hearted banter. But first I will have to wade my way through the male chauvinistic emails that will have evolved on the screen in front of me.

It's a fairly large office with four desks at the front occupied by the young lads and then in filled with tall filing cabinets and a huge work counter with photocopying machines and stationery cupboards below. At the end was my desk propping up the window space and my work colleague Amy's desk was off to the right. The boss's office door was just to the right of the work counter, he had already arrived and he was sitting behind his desk, talking on the phone, so I just offered a wave and peered in to see if Jenny his secretary was there, but she wasn't .

"Morning Tess" hits my ears from the far reaching corners of the room and I wave a sign in response.

It was Amy, grinning at me as I walked up to my desk. She seemed like a nice enough girl, though I wasn't sure about the tattoo on her nape. She had a really nice short black cropped hairstyle, but did herself no favours whatsoever in wearing a somewhat straight laced suit of navy, it just didn't do her figure any justice at all.

"Morning Amy" I smiled and started to place my mobile phone on my desk, sat down and booted up the computer in front of me.

"Don't forget you have a meeting this morning?" she offered.

"Tell me about it. I've been racking my brain all morning trying to remember his wife's name"

Amy chuckled to herself and shook her head. "Does it matter?"

"Suppose not. But you know you have to make the effort" I replied humorously.

As I searched my emails for any relevant words that will set me off for the day I started to paste lots of messages to myself in my diary to remind me of the latest posh line or statement I have just heard or read. You know the one you wish you had thought of first but someone always beats you to it. I am convinced that one day I will come up with the perfect sentence to impress all my gentleman associates and then they might take me more seriously. I think to myself 'Fat chance of that ever happening'. Today is no exception but I remember hearing a conversation between two of the men from the next office, talking about someone they knew.

"That guy's really smart you know?" said the first man.

"Yeah, what make's you say that?" replied the second.

"He's like an 'absorbent minefield of information'. He always seems to know a lot about everything" said the first. They were obviously easily impressed by another man's level of intelligence.

Thinking to myself, I must remember that, I jot it down as my new line for today's, 'must use column' and highlighted it in yellow so I don't forget. There, all I had to do is manufacture a conversation around the statement and I'd cracked it. One step further for me in the realms of smartness.

My mobile phone started to ring and I answered it quickly to avoid disturbing the others. It was my long term boyfriend at the other end checking in to fill me in with the latest news.

"Morning Tess" he said in gentle tones.

"Hi James"

"Don't forget we're going out tonight. I told them we'd be there early so I can have a quick chat with them before the others arrive. You're alright with that aren't you?"

"Yeah sure. Did you manage to find anything to wear?"

"Not yet, but I'm going into town later so I'll find something then"

"I found a brilliant skirt to wear James, you'll like it" I teased.

James starting laughing at the other end of the phone, knowing fine well I was trying to tease him with my style of dress. He knew I would deliberately find something that would set his taste buds going for the rest of the night.

"I'll be at your place for seven, okay.............Love you" he said and put the phone down, at the other end.

I didn't get a chance to say goodbye, but presumed he must have been busy with something.

He was always confident and at times had a condescending manner, but charmed the hell out of me with his amazing smile and incredible dress sense. You know the kind, you just want to stroke the silk shirt on his back and brush up against him, labelling him 'my property - hands off'. Nineteen months and three days later we had managed to standardise our lifestyle with dinner bashes, posh meals and basically entertaining his long list of clients. I began to reminisce over when we first met.

It was shortly after my 26th birthday and I was enjoying a night out with the girls. My friends and I were busying giggling over a glass of wine after finishing off a well earned Italian pudding at Portofino's, a well established Italian restaurant on the high street.

"God that was good!" chirped Anne as she licked her lips with delicious intent.

"I'm feeling stuffed now!..........how was your's Stacey?" I asked.

Stacey was busy scraping up the last of her pudding onto a spoon and proceeded to shove it into her mouth as though she was about to make love to it.

"Hmm, spot on!" she replied.

We all started to giggle and then Anne and I looked at each other and decided to repeat Stacey's silly answer with repartee.

"Hmm...........spot on!" we chanted and giggled some more.

Anne was busy weighing up the talent and spotted someone that seemed to intrigue her.

"Hey, look at mister smoothy over there!" said Anne in her usual charmless manner.

"Who…….?" I asked straining to catch a look

"No, over there. Next to the big guy" she insisted.

"Oh I see him…. No he's not really my type" said Stacey disinterested in either of the men.

But I did feel interested and started to watch him with a little too much enthusiasm.

"Ooooooh look at Tess. She's got the hots haven't you girl?" teased Anne.

"I'm just looking" I replied and it was true, I did as Anne had so eloquently put it 'have the hots!'

I liked the fact that he was distinguished looking and extremely tall. I weighed up everything about him from his well groomed, mousy brown hair to his incredibly blue eyes. He seemed quite serious, but then he showed signs of a rather nice smile. This was the one man I definitely wanted to bump into in more ways than one and decided to grade him an honourable 8/10.

"Right, here's twenty….." started Stacey as she read the bill that had just been placed on the table. "Have you got any money Anne?"

"Tell you what give me that, I'll pay on my card and then we'll have just enough for drinks later on" Anne replied, taking control of the matter.

"Here's my twenty Anne" I said, digging into my purse and handed her a folded twenty pound note.

Anne rose to her feet and moved across to the waiter to pay the bill, Stacey and I followed behind. I couldn't resist slowing down to take another glimpse at my new mission and stalled for a moment, close to where he was sitting. He looked as though he was having a meeting with the other man so I took my place by Anne's side and waited for us all to leave. I tried to be discreet as I watched him, admiring his enchanting smile. I decided to sneak a look back over my shoulder as we were leaving the restaurant. And yes, to my great pleasure I spotted him watching us with those blue eyes as we started to leave.

That same night I met him again. As the girls and I challenged our dancing skills around the well polished designer handbags, I saw him arrive into the nightclub. This time minus one colleague. We stopped to take a break from the dance floor and sat down to finish our drinks.

Whilst dousing ourselves in Bacardi and cokes, tall on the glass, there he was ordering a drink at the bar. I decided to watch him with some curiosity, just to see who he could be meeting. He looked so tall as he stood towering over the midget gems trailing the bar line. The more I observed him the more I became curious. Until in the end I caught his attention. As he was receiving his drink at the bar he spotted me staring straight at him, over the rim of my glass. I quickly looked away and felt a little silly, so I thought I would try to look as though I was paying attention to my friends.

"Hello" said a voice from behind me so I shot round to take a look.

"Oh hi…." I replied in surprise and there he was standing over me, smiling in enthusiasm. The girls started to nudge each other and smiled teasingly at him. But he resumed his stance and started to make conversation.

"Forgive me, but did I not see you in Portofino's earlier?" he asked politely.

"Yes" I replied, not really knowing what to say and offered an obliging smile to show my approval of his presence.

"I thought so; I'm James by the way"

"Tess"

I had become completing dumb struck and hoped he wouldn't get bored of my lack of conversation. He was extremely well spoken and rather well turned out. He put out his arm and ushered me over to another table to sit with him, so obviously I obliged.

"So tell me…….. Tess?" he started and offered me a seat "What was making you three laugh so much in the restaurant?"

I composed myself and waited for him to join me. I thought for a moment and observed his casual manner towards me with interest.

"Well you see………we have a system" I replied nervously and challenged him into coming back at me with the next obvious question.

"Go on" he insisted rising to the bait, taking a swig from his pint.

"We grade men!"

James suddenly sprayed his drink from his glass and nearly choked on hearing my words. I couldn't help but laugh at his reaction.

"Was I graded?" he asked curiously.

"Oh yes, you scored an eight!"

"I'm flattered" he said and laughed at my silliness. He started to relax and tell me why he had been at the restaurant.

"I was having a meal with one of my clients……" he started.

"What do you do?" I interrupted curiously, noticing how smart he was looking.

"Oh sorry, I'm a solicitor" he continued "Anyway I wouldn't normally have been there……." he suddenly stopped "By the way what did *he* get?"

"What do you mean?" I asked, puzzled by his change of direction in the conversation.

"What was his grade?"

"Oh he didn't. Stacey wasn't impressed with him" and that seemed to amuse him even more and James laughed out loud at this revelation and applauded my witticism. He continued to chat on aimlessly as the night went on. In fact that night he chatted incessantly to me for nearly two hours, for the first and last time. After that night it was my turn to do all the talking for both of us.

After a long and tedious two hour meeting I eventually managed to wave goodbye to the latest of many clients and returned to my desk. I had finally managed to clinch another deal for the firm with the usual 10% deposit, to secure a 5 year contract and that was my bonus for the month well and truly in the bag. It turned out his wife was called Cecilia not Cynthia, but I was close enough.

Gazing up at the wall clock I realised that I had missed my luncheon slot at the Taps with the girls so instead I finished off the paperwork and played catch up with the leftover pile of files, cluttering the corner of my desk. Ahead of schedule I plodded on until nearly teatime and started to close the system down on my machine. I walked over to Amy's desk to have a quick chat. I started to tell her of my plans for the evening.

"James is taking me out tonight." I started "So I'm going to skip off early doors and rejuvenate my un-manicured nails in time for this evening".

"Where to?" replied Amy, smiling; sitting back in her chair to listen.

"To a Hog roast bash apparently." I replied, whilst looking down and flicking a used staple from my skirt.

"Oh really?" she responded in a disappointed mumble and turned back to her monitor with indifference to my news.

"Yes…….. I know what you're thinking. It could be good fun" but she seemed to switch off at that point as if to she say she was no longer interested in his choice of venues, so I collected my handbag and set off home.

Chapter three

This was going to be the first time I had ever been to a cowboy bash and I wasn't really sure what I was going to wear. By the time I arrived home I had just enough time to top off my amazing all year round natural shade of orange tan. I opted for a safe yet flattering shortish suede skirt, that I had told James's about earlier and pulled on my tanned, leather boots. After all there was bound to be line dancing on the cards and I knew James's wouldn't be able to resist practicing his dancing skills for that one. It was going to be an interesting evening and I knew it was the perfect opportunity to pose alongside James, so somehow I had to choose an outfit that would tantalise him and at the same time encourage him to show me off too. I tied my pretty checked blouse into a well positioned knot, just above the belly button and curled my hair with my well used curling tongues.

James had just arrived outside my apartment and was letting himself in with his key. I heard him coming in so I popped my head round the edge of the door and greeted him in my usual charming way.

"Hi love!"

"How long are you going to be Tess?" he asked, knowing I wouldn't be ready and started picking up some of my things off my living room carpet.

"Nearly done…….honest. Two minutes tops!"

He waited patiently for me to finish adding the final touches to my hair and proceeded to give me the usual gentle reminder about how it was important to project ourselves with absolute decorum. I knew exactly what James was going to say; because he did this every single time he took me out and always saw fit to remind me that I had to behave myself. As boyfriend's go James had an irritating knack of trying to turn me into some kind of sophisticated and refined woman of substance, when in reality I am the girl at every party attracting male audiences everywhere, consuming one too many complimentary drinks at the pleasure of some unassuming host's expense. Even indirectly victimising some poor unfortunate sober gentleman with my clumsy attempts in the form of general knowledge and humour, that would leave anyone hitting the decks in laughter. No matter how I tried to master the art of decorum it just wasn't being absorbed into my silly little brain cells and nor would it if I kept enjoying the attentions of yet another gentleman's wallet. Alcohol and I had never agreed and never would.

"You will watch what you drink tonight, won't you love?"

"I'll be fine. It's only a hog roast" I replied, stepping into view and promptly gave him a quick twirl "There, what do you think?"

James smiled approvingly, came closer and proceeded to give me a nerve tingling kiss on my freshly painted lips.

"Listen…." he started and repositioned my knotted tie to cover my belly button. "These people are clients of mine and they are hoping for a good turn out tonight. I just need a couple of minutes with them to discuss some papers, okay?"

"It's never just a couple of minutes though is it? I mean, I always end up standing on my own at these places and I always have to wait for you" I argued.

"Come on Tess, it's business. Besides you're getting a night out as well aren't you?" he encouraged.

"Suppose so…" I mumbled.

"Suppose so!" he repeated teasingly and smiled at my lack of enthusiasm.

I started to examine his attire and walked a circle round him as if he was on an inspection. He smiled and laughed through his nose as I gave an approving nod of satisfaction.

"You'll do" I said nodding, whilst admiring his taste in clothes.

His strong muscular tones were showing through his well chosen plaid shirt and James had excelled himself in his latest purchase of cream chinos.

We were just about ready to leave so I grabbed my bag from off the table and checked for my keys.

"Right and you know not to say anything unless you really need to?" he continued, still encouraging me towards the door "I've been a solicitor in this firm for a good few years now and it's important that everything should go well" he urged, so I offered a look of contempt and met his eyes with one of my perfected sarcastic smirks.

Even though I was fully aware that his job was important to him and more importantly so was his social life I still felt he hadn't quite grasped the concept of taking care of me first. He had set his standards very high and tonight was going to be no exception to the rule. I hadn't eaten all day and felt in a ratty mood so at this point I decided to show him my disdain in being told how to present myself and started to pick a squabble, which later on ballooned into something straight out of a comedy sketch.

"I do know how to present myself"

"I'm referring to the alcohol Tess" James quickly fired back "You know what you're like if you drink too much" and that was the start of his prudish manner for the rest of the evening and he promptly locked the door behind us.

He had seen me become very playful many times before, usually after a couple of drinks and was in mood for one of my embarrassing scenes. When it came to drinking more than two glasses of wine I turned into the girl every conservative wife or territorial woman loved to hate. James had decided it was better that he didn't drink this time so we set off in his extremely posh Mercedes. It was a two door coupe with all the latest gadgets and gismos that money could buy. James's car was to him the next in line of many toys. He believed in his usual pretentious way that it was advertising his status to the world. I sat in the passenger seat and I could tell instantly that yet again his car interior had been valeted as it was spotlessly clean. For some reason it had to be valeted every week just in case he was going to meet one of his clients. His weekly ritual of carwashes had become a compulsory necessity over the years.

"What are you listening to?" I asked puzzled as he changed the music over.

"Listen……can you not guess?"

"No. Just tell me"

"It's James!" he exclaimed and started to laugh at my vacant expression.

"Oh very funny!"

"No seriously. Do you not remember the show at the M.E.N. arena a few months back?"

I shook my head, amused by his typical banter and listened to some more of the music until I suddenly remembered one of the songs.

"Yes……..now I remember!" I chirped up, satisfied that I had finally recognised some of the music.

James just sniggered at my forgetfulness and grinned for a second as my memory of that night came flooding back.

With punctuality at the top of the agenda for James we inevitably were the first to arrive. On entering the gateway we noticed a huge sign passing over our heads which read:

'Hog Roast Yee Ha and Apple Cider'

James parked directly in front of the entrance; I climbed out and waited as he locked the doors. He sauntered round to the front of his car and took hold of my hand and squeezed it gently in recognition of my being there for him. He smiled for a second and then we set off for the front door. He stepped back and patiently waited for me to go through to the other side.

"Now remember these clients are important to the company" James reminded me calmly and gently pushed me forwards.

"I'll try" I retorted with equal velocity and looked around to see if anyone else had arrived.

James was doing what he always did; reminding me of my place became second nature to him. His attention steered him towards the host and his wife who were waiting a little way in from the entrance.

"They're over there" he hinted and continued to take a few steps ahead of me to greet them first.

"James!" replied the bloke, who I couldn't help noticing was a little bit on the shortish side, yet decidedly quite jolly.

James shook his hand and turned to the his wife and proceeded to shake her hand too. He nodded in acknowledgement and smiled intensely, turned to the side and politely allowed me into the conservation.

"This is Tess"

"Hi" I said, not really sure of what was expected of me.

"This is Ted and Barbara Plumpton" he said, confirming our hosts for the evening.

"Very pleased to meet you Tess" said Barbara, shaking my hand.

"Like wise" said Ted gripping my hand in his somewhat sweaty palm.

"Tess, do you mind sweetheart......." James whispered into my ear "only we just need to have a little chat. Okay?"

I thought for a moment, what James actually meant was 'you can bugger off now Tess. There's a good girl!'

I walked over to the centre of the building feeling a little disgruntled in the way I had just been dismissed and left them to their own devices. The building turned out to be a huge barn which looked as though it had been extended even further to create a huge function room. As I looked round I spotted an open fireplace over at the other far end with what looked to be the hog, turning on a huge roasting spit, hanging just above it. I felt quite excited so I walked over to give it a closer inspection and to my amazement I was staring at an enormous inglenook with the largest log fire in it I had ever seen.

I was still sulking over James's behaviour towards me, so I couldn't help but visualise him becoming the latest hog to be tied to the spit. He was slowly being turned over and over and all of his body fat started dripping over the logs.

'Yes a big drip!' I thought and continued to watch the real hog roast in fascination and felt decidedly smug.

I ventured over to the long bar which was displaying all kinds of nuts and assorted snacks in wicker baskets, propped myself up onto a tall bar stool and ordered a drink.

"What are you having pet?" asked the cowboy serving.

"What do you recommend?" I asked, feeling thoroughly bored and extremely fed up with the situation.

"A cider!" was his delightful statement and he offered as a way of encouragement.

"A cider it is then" I replied, feeling more cheerful as he grinned at my sullen face.

As I began to enjoy my first drink of the evening I knew I wasn't going to be bothered with any more of James's stupid reprisals for a while, yet at the same time I wished he was by my side so I could have someone to talk to.

"See......that wasn't too long was it?" said James, pulling up a seat next to me.

"A couple of minutes you said" I replied, feeling relieved he was back with me.

James just smiled at me satisfied that he had done what he had set out to do and ordered himself a cider.

"Do you realise how long it took me to get ready?" I nagged, still miffed at his absence.

"And I bet you dressed just to impress me too? He teased, grinning.

I stared at him in disbelief at his annoying matter of fact statement. Whether or not it was true, that I had actually dressed to impress him, he had the knack of making it sound like a condescending remark.

He leaned over to offer me a peace offering and kissed me on my cheek, stepped back from his stool and pulled me over to him for a friendly hug.

"Come on then........" he said, still smiling at me "let's circulate"

As the room started to fill with men darning cowboy hats and checked shirts and their women partners with silly pigtails, tied up in gingham ribbons, James and I were busy watching them whilst soaking the atmosphere and appreciating the ambience of the place. I settled down to one or two pick me ups and waited for James to realise I was still in the room. His attention steered him towards Ted and his wife who were busy welcoming in the guests as they arrived.

"Do you want to dance?" James asked eagerly and held out his hand to guide me over to the dance floor.

"Oh, go on then"

We teamed up next to a really nice couple who had gathered other people into rows already and we observed how they started showing everyone the steps for the next dance. They were a friendly couple and they went all out to impress the other guests with their line dancing skills. A banjo band had started playing just behind them. And we suddenly found ourselves on the first row of dancers. I teamed up with James and listened to the usual recital of introductions.

"Off to the left............ heal turn ....and off we go!" came the chanting from an avid dancer.

James loved dancing and I felt really proud to be with him, especially when it was me who was messing up all the moves. James grabbed my arm and gently nudged me every time I had to turn so I could keep up with them all. He laughed and pushed his hands into his pockets and tilted his head, shifting to the right step then to the left and generally just showing off. But I knew he was doing it really well. I pulled out on the next dance to have a break and James followed behind. He was getting a real sweat on and changed his drink to sparking water to hydrate him.

An hour had passed by fairly quickly by this time; I kept nodding with a smile when ever anyone tried to speak to me as I couldn't hear a word they had said over the loud music.

"Come on, join in you two!" someone called over to us from the dance floor.

James just grinned even more when he realised we were going to have some more fun and pushed me in front of him to join the dancers. But dancing was not on the cards. This time it was lasso!

I decided to go first and wanted to impress everyone with my talent in swishing a lasso over my head, or so I thought as I had never really tried it before. As I struggled with the rope I managed to create an audience of supporters who cheered me on, which seemed to happen in all good rodeo films. The fun part of this event was that each man in turn came up and had a go. This kicked off a knock on effect with the crowds and raised some amused eyebrows. As everyone took their turns we stood back and clapped to the music allowing other people to join in and have a go.

Eventually it was time for us all to regroup and dance to the next up beat tune. Unaccustomed as I was to drinking half pints of cider I started to behave like a big kid and danced away oblivious to the correct step formation and without a care in the world. No matter how I tried, thinking that I had got the hang of it, the line of dancers quickly changed to another direction and started again. In some clumsy, haphazard way I managed to link arms with James. We stepped in line and with our other hands in our pockets we carefully followed suit. Stepping out to the right we shuffled our feet and skipped off to the left until eventually we managed to take control of our movements. In the background the band still played whilst everyone practised a chorus of yee ha's.

James and I couldn't help but notice the distinctive aroma of a roasted joint, the warm succulent smell that kindly stimulates the taste buds just like a Sunday roast dinner. We casually made our way to the front of the queue with our cutlery at the ready and holding out our empty plates the hog roast was carved before us. We filled our plates to the brim with all kinds of pickles, breads, salad and the all important meat.

As we shuffled our way up onto rows of inter connecting benches and placed our plates down on the huge slab of timber that had been turned into a banquet table everyone began to assemble and took their places next to us. We all settled down to some friendly banter.

"Hey you were pretty nifty with the lasso earlier" said a cheerful chap.

"Thanks" I replied and smiled.

"Nifty.......she near as damn it lassoed my hat clean off!" exclaimed another bloke.

Everyone in ear shot started laughing and I felt a little embarrassed, but not for long as someone decided it was James turn.

"So, I suppose you'll need to bend your knees more than the rest of us?" James sniggered at the remark that was obviously referring to his height and continued to eat a huge bite of his hog bap.

"The band's good isn't it?" I joined in trying to protect James's embarrassment.

"Oh, it is dear. Do you know they were playing at the village hall last year and they had everyone up on their feet dancing pretty much all night" replied the woman sat opposite me nodding in acknowledgement, rattling off her own thoughts on the matter.

Even though we didn't really know anyone it soon became apparent that after some gentle humour with our newly made dancing partners; Hog Roast Yee Ha was definitely a night out not to be missed. We just ate and smiled and took turns to join in on the conversation. And after our workout on the dance floor we couldn't help but devour everything on our plates, it tasted absolutely wonderful. Perhaps this was because we were so incredibly pumped up with adrenaline after all that dancing and making utter fools of ourselves or just because it was so appetising to eat. Either way my ratty mood had disappeared into a distant memory and James was back in my good books.

Before long we were feeling completely stuffed and at one with the world so we strolled over to the dance floor, wrapped our arms round each others waists from behind and continued to watch the dancers from a distance. The floor was strewn with scatterings of hay and all along the back of the walls they had stacked bales of hay rather precariously with optimum effect. The whole scene had been brilliantly put together right down to the last detail and in some ways as we looked on, we couldn't help but notice the relaxed atmosphere as people clambered onto the haystacks to recuperate. The dedication on some of the dancers faces convinced us that this was definitely a popular form of entertainment.

I reached over for another drink from the never ending supply at the bar and continued smiling at the procession of dancing cowboys and cowgirls. It didn't matter what I was drinking really, the golden rule was no more than two glasses and more importantly never on an empty stomach. By now I had certainly exceeded my limits but felt sure that after all that food I would be alright. Evidence from previous attempts to enjoy myself proved quite clear, I could not handle alcohol at any level or busy crowded rooms. I was fairly certain the barn was large enough for me not to get too hot and it definitely wasn't too crowded so chances were I wouldn't be doing any fainting tonight. I definitely didn't want to make James aware of how much I had already consumed so I slipped away from his side and sneaked off to the toilets to freshen myself up.

James was standing next to a man who had been a dab hand with the lasso earlier and suddenly noticed my absence. He took no time at all in starting up a conversation with man.

"You did well with the lassoing mate" James started.

"Yeah cheers……. I see your girlfriend's certainly enjoying herself?"

"Oh yes, she likes going to do's"

"Does she always get the giggles?"

James started to become slightly suspicious by the man's remark "Tess's just enjoying herself"

"She's obviously not used to cider though is she, eh?" the man persisted and smiled.

"No, probably not" James answered feeling sure he had missed something. So he took it upon himself to investigate further and waited for my return.

By now we were really into the night's festivities and I'd started to feel tipsy. James had seen me coming back from the toilets, trying desperately to remove a piece of toilet paper from the soul of my boot and followed closely behind. He was still on the water and completely sober and decided it was time to observe my stance for a while. He soon noticed my lack of ability to walk a straight line and began to feel disillusioned, knowing he had distinctly told me to behave myself. James was all too aware that left to my own devices I could be more than capable of making a fool of myself if he didn't take matters into his own hands and soon.

Meanwhile I was oblivious to his presence and busy taking my next swig of cider, whilst glancing over at our hosts. Not being sure where James was at this point in time I took the opportunity of going over to chat with them. I figured I should start up a conversation with them and utter a perfectly acceptable intelligent comment about expecting to see a buckaroo ride. Then I have an inspiration to start a conversation to shame all conversations……..

"Hi!"

"Oh hi Tess" Ted replied and Barbara just smiled in confirmation.

"Can you imagine what it would be like to stride a buckaroo after drinking too much?" I asked, thinking this was a perfectly good question to ask.

"No?" he replied and looked slightly puzzled and shook his head.

"Well, everyone would end up with projectile vomit all over them" I started giggling as I said it " It would be so funny wouldn't it?"

At this Ted quickly started to groan and shook his head even more.

"Oh, honestly Tess" said Barbara, covering her mouth at the prospect.

As Ted looked at his wife I sensed that this probably wasn't the best taste in conversations I could have come up with after all.

What I didn't realise was James had stood just behind me and heard my bad taste in jokes. Feeling sure that I had gone too far and had too much to drink, he took it upon himself to remove the offending problem from the room. The problem being me! At that moment I felt the full force of James's hand wrapped firmly round my arm.

"Ted, Barbara, sorry about this. She's just a bit giddy from the cider"

He made a gesture of apology to our hosts and pulled me away from their sights. Still with a firm grip on my arm he dragged me the length of the barn to the furthest corner, out of hearing range of our confused and somewhat bewildered hosts.

At that moment I felt an incredible urge to laugh and turning on my heels I stared into his beautiful eyes and with a disgustingly loud laugh I attempted to justify my train of thought on the matter.

"Oh come on James that would be hysterical though wouldn't it?"

With one glance at my glass James hesitated for a moment. He took hold of my shoulders and stared into my eyes with a disappointed gaze.

"Theresa how many have you had?"

"Whoops" I teased and started to laugh even more "James's is not amused!"

But seeing the stern look he was giving me I knew I had to try and stop laughing. He always called me by my real name when he wanted to tell me off. So with a clearing of my throat I tried to compose myself, but with little effect.

"I've only had a few! Sorry!" I whispered apologetically and attempted to snuggle into his chest for comfort and reassurance. I pulled myself in even closer and continued to offer what I thought would be a more convincing and plausible excuse, with a more thoughtful deliverance.

"I just thought they would have a sense of humour"

But James continued to look disapprovingly towards me and I knew my pleas were going to have little effect. He sighed that all too familiar note of discern and gradually pushed me away as if to consider his options. It was official; I had yet again made a complete fool of myself. James soon decided to take charge of the situation and removed the glass from my hand, placing it down on the table to his right.

"I think you've had quite enough for one night" he said taking me firmly by the hand and started walking towards the exit.

"But James……..what about…….?" but James was in no mood for any lame attempts of pleading on my part and quickly interrupted.

"I'm taking you home!"

And that was the evening cut short. James made quick work in advancing towards the exit door, dragging me ungraciously behind. I couldn't help but notice we were not just leaving, but leaving without even stopping to say our goodbyes. He made short work of our escape and proceeded back to the car, released his grip of my arm and swung me round to wait for him to open the door. James was swiftly taking me home like a naughty child and throwing me the silent treatment into the bargain with his disapproving stance over me.

He didn't speak in the car, instead he chose to give me even more of his silent treatment that was supposed to sober me up very quickly. James just drove into the night without even playing any music in the background. Just complete silence. Well except for the constant humming of the engine and occasional ticking from the dash board as he signalled left and right. Even as we came up to the traffic lights he stayed indifferent towards me. I began to feel quite nervous in his intolerance of me and observed him as he propped his arm on the window of his door. He didn't look at me for the whole journey, he just leaned his cheek into the palm of his hand as if he would rather be somewhere else and drove slowly with his left hand clutching the wheel.

Soon he pulled the car over to the curb and stopped to drop me off. We had arrived just outside my apartment and reluctantly I started to release my seat belt. James turned towards me and waited quietly for me to finish. In a calmer choice of tongue he looked at me and said:

"You need to get some sleep……I will speak to you tomorrow Tess" and as an after thought he concluded his final sarcastic remark "When you have sobered up!"

At that he leaned over and kissed my face then promptly looked forwards through the windscreen into the night beyond, as if I had just been excused. I couldn't think of a single thing to say that could appease the situation so I clambered out of the car and closed the door. James just drove off without even looking back at where I was still standing as I watched on in despair. What was worse I knew James was typically and completely sober on sparkling water and that he would be reminiscing over my bad behaviour for ages afterwards.

Within a few minutes I had managed to climb the stairs inside my apartment building and was placing my key into the lock of my front door. Once inside I closed the door behind me and switched on the light to my cosy living room. But before long it suddenly dawned on me the other problem to drinking excessive amounts. The walls of my apartment started to spin round, just the way the buckaroo would have done given half the chance. I quickly stumbled to the bathroom and in my earnest to call out for 'Hughie' down the toilet, to my amazement the bathroom door jumped out and slapped me very hard in the face. Bang!

"Aah! That one will definitely hurt tomorrow" I cried out, holding on to my sore forehead and then I found my needs even greater and out of sheer frustration I opened my bedroom window, leaned over the window ledge and Hughie was delivered from a great height, approximately two floors up, to the pavement below.

I slumped down onto my comfy couch and tried to compose myself for a while but the agony of my really bad bump to the forehead and the constant sense of feeling sorry for myself finally got the better of me. As a last resort I reached into my bag to find my mobile phone. In desperation I was calling James's mobile and waited to hear his voice at the other end.

"What is it now Tess?" he asked obviously still fed up with me.

"James?" I started miserably "I need you……. I've really hurt myself"

"What have you done?" he asked, starting to sound concerned as to my well being.

"Do you know how much I love you James………"

"Tess you're just drunk" he insisted, sighing in frustration.

"Did I ever tell you James……. how much I adore you?" I persisted in pleading, with affectionate tones.

"I thought you'd fallen down the stairs or something you silly woman" he snapped. James became silent at the other end and I worried about what he was thinking. After a few seconds his silence became unbearable so I knew I had to coax him some more if I was to get anywhere with him, knowing the mood he was in.

"I will continue to love you forever and ever if you could just come back and pick me up"

Still James kept quiet, obviously weighing up the situation so I attempted grovelling to his better nature.

"You could take me back to your place and make me better again.........
please James, please"

James listened to me in silence, then after a pause in the conversation....

"Alright, wait there and don't do anything else, do you hear?" and like a true gentleman he turned his car round and drove back to my apartment to pick me up.

Taking just one look at the state I was in he agreed to take me back to his house. He locked up the apartment and guided me back down the stairs, across the pavement to his car. After pointing his trusted gismo at the lock the car door released. He opened it and bundled me back into the passenger side. Carefully closing the car door after me James sat back in the driving seat and drove us back to his house. In a way that was so typical of him as he never really shouted at me very often and he rarely raised his voice to anyone. Most of the time he merely changed the tone in his voice to show that you had met with his disapproval. One thing I knew for sure was James had a forgiving nature especially when it came to my wellbeing. As he drove us back to his house I tried to imagine what the caption would read in my journal and came up with an idea to be pencilled in later. I thought to myself it was going to have to read something like: *'Love is - putting your girlfriend to bed smelling of sick and comatosed from a good night out!'*

By the time we finally arrived back at James's house it had already turned midnight. The obvious signs that he'd had time to calm down were evident to him, but had gone completely unnoticed by me. He quietly smiled to himself in his usual sympathetic way and sat me down long enough to prise the boots from my feet, then laid me across the sofa to rest. Before long he was comforting my bruised forehead with a bag of frozen peas to keep the swelling down and pouring hot coffee down my neck to sober me up. Conversations were still not on the agenda as James was still reluctant to let me have it all my own way and had no intentions of letting me off the hook just yet. Finally I drifted off to sleep so he carefully carried me upstairs to his bedroom. By this time my body was incapable of doing anything for itself so he unfastened my blouse and placed it on the chair neatly, unzipped my skirt and pulled it down from my worn out body and draped the quilt over me in quiet motions so as not to wake me up. He stood by the bed and observed me for a while as I slept before turning off the light and eventually he closed the door and crept back downstairs. It turned out James slept on the settee that night.

Chapter four

After a hard week I find myself skidding through the busy streets in town, to catch up with the latest gossip over lunch with my friends. It's been two weeks since my disagreement with the bathroom door. James had shown his usual self control and settled for his typical 'least said, soonest mended' method towards me and that was the last he spoke of that fateful evening. Even though I was still nursing a bruising to the head, well disguised with even more plaster of Paris in patched tones to remove the evidence of a multi coloured shade of purple forehead, I had no intentions of keeping quiet when it came to gossiping with the girls. After all they were equally as bad as me at parties and we had spent many a night reminiscing over a swollen ankle or two.

The Taps Bar was a popular haunt for all the up and come entrepreneurs and had already filled up with the latest fashion trendy guys and three inch heeled dolly brigades. The young men hung around the bar hoping to be noticed by the girl with the huge cleavage, trying to look intelligent with their crumpled shirts and the latest coffee stain down the front of their ties. I spied the girls sat tall on their high stools at the far end of the bar, the ideal opportune position to go talent spotting, poised up against the newly polished dance pole.

"Sorry I'm late" I said as I sat down and removed the cling film wrapping from my latest designer salad, the one with a sliced boiled egg, grated cheese, pasta twists and lettuce leaves.

"Oh that's alright, we've just been busy checking out the nerds" replied Anne and she promptly pointed to a bloke, walking out of the gents with his flies still undone. "See what I mean" she sniggered.

"I was starving. Sorry Tess I had to start without you" replied Stacey, looking a little bit too pleased for eating hers in my absence.

Anne was my oldest friend from school and was tucking into a lengthy baguette filled with salad and chicken pieces, doused in mayonnaise. She was the same age as me and she had an interesting shade of brunette, shoulder length hair in soft waves. Her dress sense was similar to mine and her philosophy in life was never to buy anything in the sales. If she didn't want to buy it the first time round, what on earth possessed the retailers to challenge her into believing that this time; she would be buying something for a steal. No, if it wasn't the latest colour, length or season she had her nose twitched high in total disregard. She had the same wicked sense of humour as me and delivered an unmistakable laugh that can only be matched by Muttly the dog and his accomplish Dick Dastardly, sitting in on the sidewalk.

Stacey was much more delicate with her choice of foods and had opted for some kind of spicy wrap, gift wrapped in a paper towel. She always managed to discreetly wipe away any leftovers from her lips, with a quick check in with a serviette. Stacey was a relative new comer and slightly older in years with a short, thick set crop of peroxide hair with darkened roots. Stacey shared her clothes with the latest up and coming charity shops throughout the kingdom. I'm not saying she had a lot of clothes but she always managed to be much more agreeable with the prospect of picking up a bargain designer label at the local Oxfam. As bright as she was and much more self controlled she wasn't as reserved when it came to choosing her clothes, as Anne always seemed to be. Much more educationally stimulating, prim yet dogmatic at all times, Stacey had risen to the ranks of a lab technician in a short space of time. Amazingly she had shared a house with me throughout our college days, without allowing any of her intelligence to rub off on me.

In all they were my best of friends and nothing escaped them. I sat up tall alongside them and began to tell my tales.

"I've had to stay off work so people didn't see the mess I've made to my head" I started "I only went back this week"

"Well you have to admit Tess, that's not the best excuse for getting a battering is it. No I would of chosen a more subtle approach, like say

…….Have you seen what James did to me?" teased Anne with delicious intent.

"Anne, you can't say that. Anyway he's been looking after me. I can hardly accuse him of beating me up now can I?"

"Anne's only playing with you"

"Psst…………definitely a four….look over in the corner" Anne remarked, pointing to a geek who was busy sifting through the pages of his private eye.

"Definitely" started Stacey in agreement "Anyway did I tell you about my supervisor?"

Anne and I looked at her in bewilderment as we knew all too well she hadn't.

"She's only bonking the guy from the science department"

"So…………do we know him" I asked confused.

"You wouldn't want to………anyway, he's a good fourteen years older than her" she concluded.

When it came to the mismatch of affairs in the office Stacey made it her business to know everything that was going on. She seemed happy in involving herself in other peoples affairs as she knew her relationships were always a recipe for disaster anyway. She always made a bad choice when it came to the men.

We decided to compare notes on the usual misguided members of the male species and Anne does her unmistakable impression of a man rubbing up against the office desk. Yes you guessed it, yet again in the history of all perverted injustices to woman kind she found herself staring at her boss's obsession with the edge of his desk.

"Thank god he didn't do a Mr Collins impression from Pride and Prejudice" I said and continued to laugh. "And sniff his fingers afterwards!"

"Oooooooh!" screeched Stacey in disgust.

If you think about it for a woman to do her own version of this habitual male act she would have to use the corner of her desk. I start to wonder in contemplation at the task in hand and visualise in my minds eye - crouching at the corner of my desk, legs astride straddling in a downward motion, rocking backwards and forwards to relieve myself with some gratification. Knowing fine well that in no time at all this would ultimately arrive at the same destination as an orgasm, I couldn't help pick up on those tell tale erogenous senses. Oh yeah, I can sense the peak coming to fruition at that most intimate of moments in a woman's inevitable time of arrival! Hmm I might be giving that a go then; obviously when the boss isn't watching!

Realising that once again I had allowed myself to become distracted, I quickly redeemed myself and paid attention to the latest in conversations. We finished our lunch and set off to leave, still giggling over the confabs that had just occurred, then the usual question of what to do tonight kicked in.

"Well we could meet up at my place" I suggested.

"Okay then........suits me" agreed Stacey.

"Will his royal condescending nibs be joining us?" Anne queried, choosing a well versed piece of sarcasm.

"Oh very funny. Actually he's going out tonight" I replied, knowing full well my friends weren't too impressed with the way he spoke to me at times.

"So....... a night in with my friends it is then!" said Stacey confidently.

"And it's a 'strictly no men policy'!" chirped Anne.

It was official, the night in was arranged. And it was decided that it had to be a night in with a good film, lots of wine and most importantly of all just us girls. We laughed throughout the rest of our lunch as we shared our catalogue of misdemeanours. It's easy to see how we get on so well.

Chapter five

I arrived home just in time to tidy up the ever growing heap from my apartment floor. I did my usual ritual of throwing my phone and bag onto the settee and called out for James. I'd seen his car parked further down the road and knew he had to be here. I quickly dumped my collection of goodies on to the floor in my bedroom, out of sight.

"Hi love!" I called in a charming manner.

"I'm in the bathroom"

As I stepped into my bathroom I could see he had already made good use of the shower and was busy brushing his hair into a more distinguished look, with just my bath towel wrapped around his waist.

"Very nice…suits you" I teased and gently pressed a kiss to his cheek.

"Listen …….." he started as he turned round to kiss me back "I've had an idea. Why don't I order you in some pizzas for the girls?"

"Oooooooh, love it" I replied, treating him to a sneaky slap on his behind.

He just laughed at my attempt to play with him and I rushed back into my bedroom to get undressed.

"The girls will be here soon, so will you let them in?"

"I thought I'd just leave them outside for a bit" replied James in his usual banter.

I ventured back into the bathroom and squeezed my fingers into his ribs to show my acknowledgement at his attempt of humour. He just smiled and backed away from my tickling gesture. He left me to finish getting undressed and sauntered back into the bedroom to finish dressing.

"I'll be five minutes" I said, stripping off and dived into the shower.

James came back in and promptly tutted at my display of leftover clothes on the floor.

"I'll pick them up for you, shall I" he asked sarcastically, but I couldn't hear him for the noise of the water colliding over my face.

As I started to change Anne and Stacey arrived with the evening's supply of soave, so James opened the door for them to come in.

"Oh, hello darling" said Anne, running her fingers through his hair in a teasing gesture. She was never one to behave herself when it came to speaking her mind.

"Hi James" said Stacey in a much compliant manner.

"Come on in, Tess's just getting ready" James replied smiling at the mischievous behaviour "I'm ordering pizzas so you need to tell me what you want girls"

"If I told you, would you really get it for me James?" teased Anne and waltzed over to the kitchen worktop to plonk down her new designer handbag.

James simply ignored her remark and started dialling out. He looked back at Anne and smiled at her wit, whilst waiting for the other end to pick up.

"We usually have a meat feast and a pineapple and ham one, too" replied Stacey, who had by now gone an interesting shade of red, due to Anne's suggestive behaviour towards James.

James nodded in acknowledgement to Stacey's choices and walked off back to the bedroom to place the order.

"Anne.......what do you think your playing at?" ranted Stacey, annoyed with Anne's behaviour.

"It's only James and besides, he's just a man after all" said Anne, dismissive of Stacey scorning her.

I stepped out of the bathroom wrapped in my bath towel and headed into the bedroom, where James was busy collecting his sporting leather holdall.

"Right it's done. I've ordered your pizzas and they should be here in twenty minutes, okay?" he asked and waited for the obligatory response.

I moved in on him to deliver a kiss to his face and James smiled for a second, then he grabbed the top of my towel to pull me in towards him and put his arm around my waist to pull me in tighter. He kissed me properly; as an after thought he wrapped a finger across the top of my nose and tweaked it in gentle play.

"Don't I get a thank you Tess?" he teased urging me to acknowledge his generosity and stroked my damp hair into position in a loving gesture.

"You just did" I replied, threw down my towel to reveal my contours and taunted him into staying.

James started to laugh at my naughty behaviour and I prepared to get ready for the girls night out without a care in the world. James took himself off to the door and observed my silly posing in the mirror and smirked with amusement before making a thrifty exit.

"Be good" he said and blew a charming kiss in my direction and set off to meet the lads. He was off to play his usual weekly ritual of squash with one of his colleagues, which seemed to sufficiently de-stress the events of his hectic day.

Now being good was certainly not on the agenda tonight, because that meant we would have to show decency and act with a clean image in our hearts, in our choice of entertainment. And that just wouldn't do when it came to the girlies.

Anne and Stacey had kicked off their shoes, a compulsory requirement for what was yet to come. Stacey was busy fumbling around with my music system and had already turned the music up. As I joined the girls I spotted Anne had already opened the first bottle of wine and was pouring it into three glasses on the worktop.

"Oh, so you are going to be joining us then" Anne teased and handed me a glass of wine.

"Hi Tess........the pizzas haven't arrived yet" chirped Stacey.

With our glasses filled we made haste on shifting the furniture round to give us more room. So the settee was pushed forwards, to allow us more room at the back to do some playful dancing later on.

"Pizzas!" exclaimed Stacey as she heard the door bell chime.

"I'll get it" I said and grabbed for my purse, out of the bag, still lying on the settee.

"Stacey, if you get some plates............" started Anne, but she was interrupted.

"Who needs plates, we'll just eat out of the boxes silly"

"Fine........if that's how commoners eat, so be it" Anne taunted, knowing she was would wind Stacey up

"You can be such a snob when you want to"

"Right, who ordered the pineapple?" I asked unaware of the row that was emerging between my friends.

We all scrambled to the floor just like commoners and scoffed the whole lot in less than five minutes, making good use of the kitchen roll to wipe our smudged faces. Anne and Stacey grinned at each other as if they were concluding the argument in their own secret way and shifted the empty boxes into the kitchen.

I turned up the volume on the music system and we got to work on our dancing skills in erotic motions. If you position yourself well you can arouse all good settees in the best possible of taste. Shimmering down and side to side with our hips swishing, we crouched further, further and further down the back of the settee until we arrived at a physical state of complete giddiness on the floor. Then Anne moved around to the side and teased the arm of the settee with her bottom, singing cheers as her cheeky moves were being brushed along to the music. Each of us were taking turns to pose for the latest imaginary six pack godliness that hadn't made our acquaintances yet. With our imaginations up and running and door frames at the ready we giggled and pole danced our way round the doorways, to imply that we were the next best thing in seductive entertainment.

As we settled ourselves down, giddy from all the laughing, we started to tidy up the place and took charge of the next saga for our evening's pleasure. The mood was set with massive throws over the back of my huge settee and lined it with dozens of overcrowded cushions from my bedroom.

"It's ready!" called Stacey as she came out of the kitchen with hot melted chocolate in my amazing new fondue.

Marshmallows at the ready with giant sized skewers and melted chocolate, which had been simmering for a while on the kitchen hob, we were ready for a 'night in' in front of the box, watching our favourite goddess's parade themselves in their American city slick show.

"How can any woman be mad enough to change her religion for her boyfriend for god's sake?" retorted Stacey as she watched the screen in disbelief. "The man can't even be bothered to turn off the tele for her. Look! She's even spent all day preparing a meal for him and he's sat there, watching the sodding box!"

Anne and I started to laugh at the way Stacey dramatised her statement with her elongated finger waving frantically at the tele. As the plot progressed Stacey settled down and stretched out across the floor and dipped yet another marshmallow into the melted chocolate. Anne and I had positioned ourselves either end of the settee with outstretched legs jumbled up in the middle, wafting our glasses into the air as we leaned forward to capture those possible glimpses of the latest sex toy.

"She's brilliant isn't she?" exclaimed Anne "I wish I could get a life sized poster of my boyfriend, looking like that"

"What....... Naked?" I giggled.

"And holding nothing more than an empty coke bottle. I should say so......... ooh yeah!" Anne let out the loudest of laughs and we all agreed.

I couldn't help but notice how quiet Stacey had become and could only put it down to the fact that she hadn't had a boyfriend in a while. Even her choice of conversations had become irrelevant to us. All I could think of was when women spend all their time poking their noses into other peoples business, it usually meant that much not much was going on in their own life.

"Are you okay down there?" I enquired

"Yeah........I've got all I need down here thanks" she giggled and I knew Stacey was okay.

We spent the rest of the evening glued to the episodes, giggling and chattering away until we'd run out of wine. Anne gave us her full account of her new found admiration for Richard and his taste in boxers or should I say lack of.

"Playboy...... I ask you. Black boxers with a pink bunny, does he really think that's sexy?" Anne said, obviously quite drunk.

"Oh I don't know............. you see these women wearing nothing more than playboy bikinis at rich men's houses....... playing volley ball" I remarked with some enthusiasm "They show it on the films all the time, don't they?"

"That's different" she scoffed "If Richard was that rich I'd be playing volley ball wearing a playboy bikini........ Mind you, if he turned up in those boxes I'd still have to disown him!"

"Aah don't be like that" I said trying to stick up for the man.

"Look, he's not exactly packing a six pack these days. More like cellulite wrapped round a torso, just passed it's sell by date" Anne finished. She always knew how to insult someone.

Not wanting to get caught up in Anne's ritual of sarcastic remarks I settled back down to listen to Stacey's rendition of man troubles. From there we heard the miserable version of Stacey's attempt to push a self destruct button on her all too long listed catalogue of failures.

"I don't know what it is....." she started "but for some reason, in my ineptitude for choosing the right member of the male species, I always seem to pick up the big drip, geek.......... Or worse the nerd!"

"Well I thought the last one was nice" Anne appeased.

I looked over at her suspiciously as it wasn't at all like her to be quite so pleasant.

"Nevertheless, I am still determined to pursue all types with vengeance!" continued Stacey in determination of her convictions.

"Go girl!" said Anne, still choosing to be nice.

"I know that eventually I can and will find that right box to tick" concluded Stacey, looking half cocked. Her head slumped down, which confirmed my suspicions. Yes she was definitely drunk.

"I've been thinking…" said Anne thoughtfully . "As boyfriend's go, Richard certainly has a knack of arousing my imagination" and sniggered to herself in contemplation "……and much to my delight!"

I wasn't sure where that comment came from, but could only presume she was feeling guilty for bad mouthing him earlier.

"You won't believe the choice of venues that Richard has come up with, for us…… to establish a more intimate relationship in. Well I mean given half the chance anyway" Anne concluded looking at her empty glass in disappointment.

The final piece of the jigsaw puzzle always concluded with me, reciting the latest of corrective declarations from James's long list on 'how to behave one's self in public'.

"He told me the other day that if I say nothing, this guy would presume I'm more intelligent than I really am"

"He would say that, he thinks he's better than you girl….and he's not you know?" said Stacey in sympathy to my plight.

"So do you reckon that's a compliment or do you think it's an insult?"

"Oh Tess! Reality check darling. You are too nice for him, isn't she Stacey?" replied Anne, fed up with the whole thing.

Stacey nodded in agreement, but I knew she had already switched off to rest of the world. She had pulled herself up against the arm of the settee to get more comfy. Whilst observing her straightening out her legs, I gently pulled a couple of cushions off the back of the settee and passed them down to her. Anne gave me an accidental boot with her foot so I decided it was about time I joined Stacey and grabbed another cushion and sat down next to her.

"He just fills me with confidence you know….." I continued, trying to fathom out what it was that made me like James so much "but then I feel…..oh I don't know, just stupid"

"Be yourself girl. Yeah….sounds good to me" said Stacey, desperately trying to stay awake.

We always ended our nights with a good old fashioned girly confession, as though it was good for the heart and soul. All I did know was that we had enjoyed ourselves like this many, many times, sharing our most intimate thoughts and fears with each other and passing judgement on the men, just for good measure and tonight had been no exception. But I still felt for Stacey as she was not herself tonight. It was as though she had lost her sparkle. There are times when you share your good fortune with your friends and there are times when you have to be there for them just to listen.

I felt a rap to the top of my head and looked up to find Anne had tipped her empty glass and clipped me over the head. Anne was dropping off to sleep.

"Tess, what do you think's wrong with me?"

"Nothing why?"

Stacey looked up to see if Anne was properly asleep.

"Do you think she can hear us?" she whispered.

"Anne's too busy counting sheep. Come on, talk to me" I insisted, gently coaxing her to release her deepest thoughts and emotions.

"It's just, I see you having the best time ever with your James and Anne's making it with Richard at every landmark she can think of…….."

I quietly laughed at her witticism towards Anne's sex life and waited patiently for her to continue.

"I don't know what I'm doing wrong" she said confused "I can't tell Anne, you know what she's like?"

"Maybe you're just trying too hard. If you just relax more and stopped looking maybe you will find Mr Right"

"It's just well… you have a good job and a posh boyfriend, Anne's got her posh job in the glossy magazine trade *and* a flashy boyfriend……. me I'm just a lab technician" she concluded feeling thoroughly sorry for herself.

"Just a bloody clever lab technician you mean?" I offered encouragingly.

The only thing for me to do now was the next best thing a friend could do. I put my arms round her and gave her a really big hug. No amount of trying to convince her that she was as normal as the rest of us was going to make any difference. Especially not after all that wine!

Chapter six

I love weekends, but today I found myself battling with a broken windscreen wiper as the rubber had started to come away. It scratched an annoying sound across the screen as I drove through the streets, but there was nothing I could do. The sky was thick with foggy rain, showing all the signs that winter was on its way. I pulled up outside James's house just in time to beat off the advances of a dirty, yellow mini that was coming the other way, towards the last parking space for yards. With smug satisfaction in the knowledge I wouldn't be ruining yet another pair of shoes by stepping into yet another manhole sized puddle; I clambered out of my car. Locking it I turned and quickly hurled myself through James's front door.

Inside there was that distinctive aroma of percolated coffee on standby and kicking off my shoes I nudged the door shut behind me. The rooms were sparse with furnishings but exceptionally clean and tidy, just the way James liked it. Unlike my cluttered apartment, everything had its place and he even managed to hang his pictures on the wall instead of on the floor like mine. With an impromptu kiss James carefully handed me my favourite mug full to the brim with piping hot coffee and followed behind me, picking up my scrunched up raincoat from where I just dropped it and hung it up beside the door. In my usual charming fashion I slapped a kiss straight onto his lips, tickled his ribs from behind and sauntered over to the designer leather suite and promptly crashed down to deliver my latest saga in great detail.

"The rubber has come off one of wipers"

"Oh, has it dear?"

"And it's raining......." I continued as I started sipping my coffee "all you can hear is the scratching on the windscreen!

"You'll have to get it fixed then"

"Obviously. What are you reading?"

"What?" he asked, looking up from his paper as if he had just been rudely interrupted.

"I said......oh nothing"

James just smiled over his paper and resumed his train of thought on the print in front of him.

After a short time I was feeling decidedly grumpy. I couldn't quite put my finger on it, but for some reason I found myself disapproving of James's lack of enthusiasm towards my ever riveting and pointless choice of conversations. As I lounged around his house in my comfiest baggy sweater and jeans, swigging my coffee, he attempted to educate me with the latest bundle of newspapers.

"Did you know the Morgan's have just sold their business for four million?" he asked as though I knew who the Morgan's were in the first place or even cared for that matter.

"Riveting" I replied totally indifferent to his choice of topics and promptly picked up a glossy magazine to mull over.

"They're one of our best clients....." he continued, then pushed the corner of his paper down to look at me "oh honestly Tess. I really worry about you sometimes"

"What, I don't know them do I?"

He shuffled his paper about just to show his disappointment in me and I sat watching him in his stimulated pose. As my thought waves started to wander, I pictured James… 6 foot tall, wearing nothing but his embossed bib and darning an extremely large nappy with a giant sized 9ct gold nappy pin through it refusing to be weaned from his silver spoon on to a pallet of articulated puree. At only three months old he's sat bolt upright in his surprisingly large highchair; he's being groomed in the art of elocution and having his whole childhood mapped out for him, training in the academic world of Latin, German and sciences, using his favourite wax crayons.

"If you read more Tess you'll have a better understanding of the world; you should take a look at this……" He walked over and presented the newspaper to me and ushered me towards the article he left by my side, opened at the relevant page of interest. 'Here we go again' I thought.

"I'm not sure I really need to know about this"

"Just read it silly" insisted James and walked back to the kitchen to refill his coffee.

As he set the oven for lunch to receive a 'bagged up' garlic bread and meat feast pizza, I tricked him into the sense of a job well done. All I had to do was position the appropriate newspaper in such a way so I could carry on flicking through the pages of my favourite glossy magazine and he wouldn't be any the wiser.

Then he started up a chapter that no man should ever engage in.

"Tess? You know I can't help but noticing you've been in an indifferent mood this morning. You don't think it's that time again do you?"

And there it was, the typical condescending approach to women's' rights to having a *normal* mood swing. Why is it they always presume everything's alright, it's just her damn period again?

"I'm reading" I answered, pretending to ignore his comment. But in his own haphazard way he took it upon himself to keep pursuing the inevitable line of enquiry.

"The monthly cycle of 28 days is just around the corner pet" he teased, laughing gently with an obvious lack of concern for my feelings.

"What?…….. Oh sorry James. I've nearly finished the article" I replied pretending to be indifferent, still scanning the pages of my well disguised magazine.

Suddenly I sensed his presence as I attempted to turn another page over. He had sneaked up behind me and caught a glimpse of what I was really up to.

"Yes I can see you've really enjoyed my article then……" he started and quickly dragged my magazine out from it's hiding place "Hmm let me see, ah yes…… fascinating!"

I kneeled across the back of the settee and tried to grab the magazine from his hands, but he just turned away to continue taunting me some more.

"It says here she's lost three inches from her waist and she still wearing double D's....stimulating read!" he taunted, laughing at my embarrassment.

"Well what do I know about investments and.........and trademarks anyway?" I ranted, fuming at him for catching me out.

"Yes it's definitely your monthly cycle, isn't it sweetheart?" he replied amused by lack of humour and promptly chucked the magazine on to my lap.

It was just so typical of James as he couldn't think to say 'it's a period' like everyone else. Why he couldn't just say *period* instead of going round the flipping houses I couldn't fathom out, but what I did know was he was definitely getting on my nerves. By this time I really wanted to pick an argument with delicious torment in mind, by pointing out his obvious faults and hugely exaggerate them just to make me feel better. But he stepped in and ruined my chance of a comeback with total calm in his voice and executed a well polished choice of words.

"Your last attempt to have an argument with me proved to be nothing more than a PMT experience" he started "you should know that I have grown to understand you when you're like this" and set out to reassure me that according to his calculations, he was going to be right.

I jumped up from my seat and for a few seconds I desperately tried to sieve through the many clip postings in my head and remembered the ultimate of all insults, or so I thought and shouted back at him in total indignation.

"You Jumped Up, Pompous Asshole!"

James wasn't usually easily shocked by anything I had to say and today was going to be no exception. As he slightly raised his eyebrows towards me he smiled and quietly sat back down to read his paper. For a few seconds he started to laugh to himself at my lame attempt of verbal diarrhoea and shook his head in amusement. At that I stormed off into the kitchen to refill my empty coffee mug and sulked in silence. I began to feel really indignant in the knowledge that a man could assume every argument a woman ever has with him can be logged down as a legitimate source of evidence, according to his calendar for the past six months.

But sure enough today was going to be no exception to James's stupid pompous train of thought. My period kicked in later that afternoon and much to his pleasure he'd won again. As I tried to lick my war wounds James beckoned me over with his arms outstretched, not completely immune to my emotions and obligingly I responded to his charms as he cuddled me in a softening embrace.

"Better now?" he asked tenderly and proceeded to massage my back with his strokes.

"Hmmm, I'll think about it. You really can be cruel you know?" I replied, still trying to sulk with little effect.

"So a quick romp's out of the question then?" he teased, so I stepped back from his chest and slapped him on his arm, just to show I wasn't amused by his poor taste in witty remarks.

But James just laughed and pretended to rub his arm better. "I'll take that as a no then, shall I?" he persisted, still laughing.

That night I decided I would crash at James's place, even though he had taken great pleasure in taunting me for most of the day, I still needed him to console me. After some gentle undoing we had managed to giggle our way through an old favourite film of Private Benjamin on the tele. Normally I didn't wear anything except a smile in bed, but I knew I had to be more discreet given the circumstances. So I opted for one of his many designer shirts instead, dragged it over my head and headed off to the bathroom. As I looked in the mirror I suddenly realised that the shirt was far too big for me and laughed at my reflection as it made me look as though I had actually shrunk in size.

I gathered my thoughts as I lifted up James's quilt and clambered into his king sized bed. I could see James's wonderfully toned body and slim physic, through the gap in the bathroom door, wearing nothing more than his kecks as he cleaned his teeth in the mirror.

"Have you cleaned your pegs yet Tess?"

"Yep!…….done it already, thanks"

I took up my pen and decided to insert one of many thoughts of the day into my diary. After some deliberation I started to write - '*Love is forgiving your man for his many faults, no matter how annoying they may be*'. Pleased with my notes I returned my book to the edge of the bedside table, as James got in alongside me.

"What are you writing......"

"Just some notes, nothing important" I replied and snuggled further down under the quilt.

"I take it you want me to put the light out then?"

Feeling the way I did, after today's constant torments, I was not in the mood for his witticism anymore, so instead I sat back up again to rectify the argument.

"No, it's fine......I will turn the thing off" I replied, starting to reach for his lamp.

He pulled me back towards his chest and started to tickle my ribs in a playful embrace.

"I'm just playing with you silly......come here!" he said, kissing me on my cheek.

I really loved him when he played with me like that. James started gently tweaking my shoulders in a massaging tease, he kissed the side of my face again and placed his hand around my rib cage to pull me in even further.

Finally we snuggled down for the night beneath the covers, as I warmed up against his radiating body. James reached out towards his bedside table and leaning over, he switched off the lamp.

Chapter seven

 ovember is a strange month. I'm peering out of my office window, watching the people rushing into their respective workplaces and I am sat here trying to remember the latest statement or one liner to add to my ever expanding 'must use column'. And it struck me that only a few days earlier I had seen the perfect phrase. I had sneaked a peak into one of James's files, as you do just out of curiosity of course, whilst waiting for him in his office.

I visualised that very afternoon in my minds eye and smiled in contentment. I had perched myself in the usual tantalising way at the front of his desk in my latest two piece suit, waiting for him to return. This was the suit I absolutely had to buy because it cried out to me, from the plastic dummy that couldn't carry it better than I would. It had a thigh length jacket with matching thigh length skirt and came in a very flattering shade of mushroom grey. I had finished it off with a complimentary if not revealing, yet simple crossover silk cream blouse, draped with long stringy lengths of costume pearls.

With my legs crossed and outstretched, shimmering in a golden shaded tan, that had the latest extracts from some exotic fruit, I had leaned back and positioned myself gracefully. I couldn't help but peer into one of his files labelled *Private*. I remember thinking it wouldn't hurt to take a peak, so I did! And there it was. It was the perfect antidote for any budding, fair skinned beginner who just wanted to improve her vocabulary. James had written in his document:

'here are my salient points of contention'

"Flipping heck that's one almighty mouthful!" I said out loud and quickly remembered where I was.

Astonished by his brilliant choice of words I rapidly scribbled it down on the back of a used envelope. He must have eaten half an encyclopaedia for breakfast to come up with that one! At that moment I heard James's voice becoming louder as he drew nearer to the door. I could hear him talking in the next room, with a discerning voice of authority.

"Irrespective of our client's circumstances, this is how we are going to play it" he said and at that I quickly let go of the cover to his file and assumed the position of all positions with some accuracy, to arouse his attention.

My train of thought was suddenly interrupted when my mobile phone decided to vibrate and dance across the desk. I looked down and saw Stacey's name flashing back at me.

"Happy birthday for tomorrow" she screeched in an excitable tone.

"Thanks" I replied and continued in a disillusioned and miserable tone "James isn't taking me out you know. He's got some rugby match to go to with his mates in Edinburgh and then they're sleeping over. I won't see him 'til Sunday."

"Aah....... that's not on. I tell you what we'll all go for drinks after work. No wait, I don't think I can manage that. Better still we can go out all by ourselves, just the three of us tomorrow. What do you say......... that will cheer you up won't it?"

I agreed and it was settled. The next day was going to be an eventful birthday after all, an enjoyable time out with the girls.

With that in mind I re-jigged my thoughts back to the matter at hand and started to raid my handbag. There it was, the tell tale signs of a crumpled, used envelope with my scribblings on the back. I entered the words into the column and highlighted them in yellow in my usual style and settled down to do some work. As I checked my never ending in-tray I spied my boss in heated discussions with one of the men in the office.

"Don't think! Just do what I damn well pay you to" He shouted, from a distance.

The last time I heard him in a mood like this; he had just done ten rounds with his wife and lost. He wasn't particularly tall, just of average height and build really with a mess of brown and grey tinged hair. I reckoned he must be in his forties by now as his children were in their teens and constantly sponging off him for something or other. His dress sense lacked in the imagination department, just a navy off the rail store suit with typical whitish shirts. He generally projected a pleasant enough temperament but today he was in no mood to suffer fools. Holding a file firmly in his hand he started to walk towards my desk and peered down at me. He slapped the file down in front of me to get my attention and I sat back in my seat, waiting for his next move.

"What's this?"

"I've spoken to Mr Carter and the only slot he has left is at the end of the month" he replied in a less bitter tone than he had just been using on the other member of staff. "You'll have to travel to London and meet him there. He's booked a luncheon appointment and pencilled you in for later that day. Now don't forget Tess, he's very important to us…. so don't mess this up!"

At this he continued to tap his finger onto the top of the file, which was still lying on my desk and said "Jenny will organise the hotel booking, oh and don't forget to keep your receipts if you want to claim them back on expenses. Okay?"

He strolled back to his office without even waiting for my reply and looking back over his shoulder; he signalled back at me with a thumbs up gesture and shouted.

"Cheers!"

I decided to read through the file in front of me, which had a note attached to the front of it telling me exactly the same thing that my boss had just conveyed to me. Shuffling myself back up in my seat, I opened the file and brought myself up to date with the man's company details and wrote little notes alongside it. My first note read 'Mr Andrew Carter' and I started to underline his name as if it was supposed to appear of some importance to the job at hand. It turned out he had his own business and he was 32 years of age. I read a bit further only to find he was now a Director of a group of companies.

After about half an hour I closed his file and collected my thoughts. I had never been to London, so if I planned this out well I could afford some 'me time' in the shops for afters. This was one trip I was definitely going to be looking forward to.

What I didn't know was James had called in the assistance of my good friend Anne, to help him pick out a birthday present for me and was at this very moment trampling through the streets of town. James had pitched himself a spot right outside a bookshop window and was peering in.

"I could buy her a book?" he called out optimistically, questioning the idea, as Anne busied herself in the next shop window.

"Boring!" she replied, totally unimpressed by his suggestion and continued to gaze at the window display.

"No…not boring Anne, just educational" he argued in his defence, disappointed by her lack of enthusiasm.

"Well…………" Anne teased "if you're looking for something educational you're looking in the wrong window"

James wasn't used to shopping with Anne and felt slightly suspicious of her intentions. He looked across at where she was standing and began to notice that something had definitely caught her eye. Sighing at the prospect of having to walk away from his first choice, he took the decision to saunter over to Anne's window.

"Well……this could educate your taste buds" she teased again whilst still admiring the view.

"Anne honestly, I meant something……….oh never mind." he sighed disapprovingly as he stared at the window display she had chosen and it turned out, Anne had pitched her spot right in front of a lingerie shop window and was pondering over the prospect of buying a tantalising bra with buckles and chains draped over it, which was now being displayed for the whole world to admire and she quickly made the decision to amuse herself further at James's expense.

'Deliciously kinky' Anne thought, smiling ambitiously and proceeded to push poor James into the shop.

As James walked round the displays he felt uneasy at the prospect of having to pick something up from the stands, whilst Anne had no problem at all and quickly busied herself in the slinky knickers section. She couldn't resist embarrassing James, especially when she observed how nervous he had become. So she felt it was her duty to assist him in all the decision making. She picked up a see through two piece set and raised it high, for him to take a look at.

"How about this?" she teased and watched how James started to go red in the face with embarrassment.

"No, put it back!" he insisted and turned his back on her as if to make her disappear.

But telling Anne to put something back didn't help James at all. In fact it made her more determined to have some fun. And worse, when James turned round he realised he was standing in front of another woman, who had just been admiring a bra that she had brought up to her chest. Needless to say she wasn't very impressed on seeing him staring at her. James had managed to embarrass himself and felt hugely indignant when she gave him a stern look as she stormed off.

"Sorry" he called after her "I didn't mean to......." but he was stopped short.

"Oh darling........look at this" called Anne, revelling in her foolishness.

Poor James turned back to see what she was up to now and sure enough she had picked out yet another sexy garment for him to admire. He decided to nip this in the bud once and for all and quickly walked over to her to have words. Anne was still beaming in her own mischievous way.

"Look......." he started "Do you have to embarrass me?"

"Oh, not your size?" she asked knowing fine well it wasn't and carried on browsing round for a bit longer.

But Anne knew exactly what to buy me and plunged for the ultimate in lingerie . She picked up yet another garment and shoved it up, towards poor James.

"How about...........this!"

Not daring to look up, given Anne's mischievous antics, he sighed and took the plunge. To his amazement he realised she'd stopped fooling around and was actually surprised in her choice.

"Oh, that's actually quite nice"

Anne had chosen a simple bustier that met with James's approval. He looked at it for a second and tried to figure out whether or not it would meet with my approval. He knew that if he didn't choose now Anne would make his life a misery.

"Yes, you're right. I think she would go for this" he nodded and smiled at Anne in agreement at her choice.

"Good, well..... all we have to do is get the shop assistant's attention, so we can get Tess's right size" Anne decided that she hadn't finished with James just yet and set about humiliating him just a little bit more, so she shouted out for the assistant to come over.

"Excuse me?" she called "Could you tell me if this is the right size?"

James felt himself becoming embarrassed again and decided to look down, doing his usual fidgeting as the young assistant stepped over to help.

"He can't decide which size would fit best" Anne continued, smirking in satisfaction and pointed directly at poor James. He tried to smile and turned to look in another direction.

Anne was enjoying every minute of this and she took great pleasure in watching him squirm as the assistant checked the label in the bustier.

"I think you may prefer a 14 miss" the girl instructed "would you like me to check for you?"

"Oh, I'm sure that James would like to buy something....... a little more restricting. Wouldn't you James?" Anne had relished in the utterly brilliant comeback she had just served. "You'd prefer a twelve wouldn't you darling?" but James was having none of it. He was convinced that Anne had had quite enough amusement out of him for one day and started giving her a stern look.

But Anne wasn't easily intimidated by James and proceeded to conclude the business of buying the bustier. She was thoroughly pleased with her triumph but hadn't quite finished with James just yet. So she decided to try his patience just one more time. As she looked around for a couple of seconds it dawned on her what her next mission should involve. It suddenly became obvious. All Anne had to do was find the matching knickers and that would finish him off quite nicely.

James was getting suspicious by this time and knew Anne was still up to something. He decided to follow her movements and on seeing what she was up to he decided finally, enough was enough. He snatched the bustier and the knickers from Anne's hands and quickly walked over to the counter to pay his bill, only to find he had to wait in a queue.

"Well done Anne! You're welcome James!" she shouted after him, but he ignored her wicked sense of humour and plonked them down on the counter.

Anne was satisfied that she had done her job well and stood back to admire her handy work; she folded her arms, giggling in amusement at his performance and waited for him to pay the bill. James wasn't impressed with Anne's performance and wasn't in the habit of letting someone get the better of him, so before allowing his patience to run out altogether he tried to cut short the shopping trip.

"Right well, thanks for your help"

"Oh but James, surely you'll need me to help you pick some flowers for her or something?"

"No really, I can manage from here thanks" he replied trying not to sound too rude "Besides, I'll have to get back and wrap these" and with that he quickly shot off back to his offices, before she could come up with anything else.

After a usual mundane shift at the office I usually like to swap into my trusty scruffs and slob around the apartment, so I set to work on making good of use of my CD collection, to set the mood for the night. But no sooner had I sat down to have a rummage through the boxes, a key was turning in the door lock and James was letting himself in.

"I didn't know you were coming round?"

"Love you too, Tess" and slowly walked up to render me a tender kiss. I couldn't help notice that he was holding his hand behind his back and I stood observing his movements for a second. He had managed to place one hand round my waist and the other disappeared out of sight, which started to puzzle me.

"What are you hiding James?"

"Well, you know I'm really sorry for not being here for you tomorrow don't you?"

I felt a sudden excitable tingling sensation rushing through my body in anticipation.

"You've bought me something" I shrieked and tried to search behind his back.

But James just laughed at my childish attempts and raised his hand above my head, to keep me waiting a bit longer.

"Aah please, let me" I pleaded as he taunted me with his playfulness.

"What do I get first, Tess?" he pointed his finger at me, forcing me to behave.

"A thick ear, if you don't give it me!"

"I meant a kiss!" and started to walk away. He was smirking in satisfaction, but I hadn't noticed.

I made the quickest decision ever, in just one second I was wrapping my arms around his neck, kissing him frantically to make him pay attention. This did the trick and he was soon sitting me down to show me my present. I quickly opened it as efficiently as I possibly could, by tearing the paper to shreds and held up the new underwear and was really impressed in his good taste.

"James......you bought this for me?"

"Well actually I have a confession to make. I asked Anne to help"

"Anne helped you to pick these, good girl!" I exclaimed still admiring her good taste in underwear "I love it......thanks James"

I hugged him as hard as I could to show my appreciation. He smiled satisfied in the fact he had got something right for me. He hadn't wanted to leave for Edinburgh knowing I was fed up on my birthday.

"She's quite a character, isn't she......... Anne I mean?"

"Why, what do you mean?" I asked, still admiring the goodies.

"Going shopping with her is like, well.....sacrificing yourself to the wolves"

I looked at him in surprise, then thought about it for a second. For James to say anything derogatory about my friends meant she had to have got up to something.

"Go on, what did she do?"

"Let's just say, she got her money's worth out of me in that bloody underwear shop"

I could tell James was not amused and it dawned on me, knowing how sarcastic Anne could be, that James must have been very brave to go anywhere with her.

James stood up to say his goodbyes and waited for me to join him, I hesitated for a moment, knowing fine well I didn't want him to go.

"But I haven't tried them on for you yet, please stay a bit longer.…it won't take me long?" I pleaded, tugging at his shirt suggestively.

"Oh I'm sorry Tess. I've still got a million and one things to sort out before I leave" he said apologetically, but he could see the disappointment written all over my face.

"Listen, I promise you…….I couldn't think of anything nicer than seeing you in this corset. Sunday night…… you can wear it for me then okay?"

"Okay"

I hugged him as close as I could, determined not to let him go just yet. He gently brought my face up to meet his and kept hold of my chin, offering me encouragement. "Promise!" he persisted and reluctantly I had to agree and offered him an obliging smile.

I went to bed that night in the knowledge that he had sacrificed himself, not so much to the wolves but to Anne and he'd done it just for me, which had to be a fate worse than death for any member of the male species. He told me she'd had her money's worth out of him and I believed him!

Chapter eight

The girls and I had arrived at the local night club to celebrate my turning 28 years of age. We had taken a taxi to save our shoes and talked our way into the club without having to pay on the door, by teasing and joking with the doormen into a lie about my age. Straight in front and slightly off to the left lay the most elongated bar ever, affording some space at the end for the staff to get up and dance, as they occasionally did. The first glasses of wine were being poured and we started to enjoy my birthday bash. We started to look round the place to check out the competition.

"Anne's turned up the stakes tonight in her shimmering top, hasn't she?" Stacey remarked.

"I had my eye on a pair of those Marc Cain tight fitted lycra's, the other day" I confirmed, admiring how the thin legged trousers had accentuated Anne's long legs. She'd topped them off with a dangling silver chain belt and black ankle boots with dozens of buckles attached and extremely high heels.

"Anne?" I shouted "Where did you get those boots?" and she smiled at my admiration for her boots and busied herself with checking out another girl's dress sense.

Stacey had opted for a short black fake leather skirt and sequined halter neck top, with three inch heeled, diamante styled strappy shoes. I had the inspiration to wear a pair of skimpy faux suede shorts with an over exaggerated gold buckled belt, which draped in an oversized position across my hip. My black and gold top stopped just below the bust line and fastened round the back with strands of blackened cords, criss-crossing into falls.

"I just had to wear these strap on shoes" I told Stacey as I tripped up on the heels. I had fallen in love with them and found it a compulsory necessity to buy them. Maybe it was the gem stones covering them which I liked so much.

To the right of us was a well polished dance floor with a DJ booth slotted over to the side, hidden behind a glass screen. Behind the dance floor were the hidden cubicles of well worn couches, not particularly well lit, to give maximum effect for that last of the evening snog. Just around the other side were the all important toilets and at the far end, looming in all its glory, was a huge richly painted swirling staircase.

"Come on girls, let's check out the scene upstairs" Anne said as she ushered us towards the staircase.

So Stacey and I agreed and started to follow Anne up the stairs. Upstairs was known as the toffs section comprising of yet another bar and an eating bistro to the far corner. We stayed upstairs for a while to do our usually posing and peered over the banisters. It was a perfect viewing spot, down to the dance floor. It was still too quiet on the dance floor so we watched as the bodies started to fill the spaces below. The general rule was that if you wanted drinks for the rest of the evening then upstairs was the most obvious place to be. Anne spotted her little squirt of a brother Dave walking in with his friends, all clambering towards the already busy bar. I say little because that's what he was, but not any more.

"Hey Dave!" she shouted and amazingly he heard her. He looked up to us and smiled.

"Hi sis!" he shouted and waved over to us as his friends took their place in the queues.

I started to remember him as a little boy and all the nights he used to peruse his long list of dinosaur books, looking for the meanest of carnivores. He was always claiming to be an authority on extracting DNA from mosquitoes embedded in amber, that we all knew he had just picked up from a scene in a Jurassic Park film. I remembered how he used to chip away at the garden rockery with his Dad's chisel; in the vane hope of discovering the latest fossil.

"Come on" urged Anne "Dave will buy us some drinks"

So we retreated back down the long staircase and signalled to the lads that we were going to sit down. We walked in the direction of the cubicles and sat down on some occasional seats, round the back of the dance floor. As Dave gathered up his first drink of the night he came over to us. No longer a little squirt, I couldn't help but notice how handsome he had become. Even though he drove a clapped out French heap of junk which scored him a measly 4/10 for effort, he struck a considerable 8/10 for good looks. And soon his friends made their way over to where we were sitting.

Each one of Dave's friends sauntered over to impress us with their latest idea of stimulating conversations and poor taste in jokes. As one leaned over towards me I picked up on that all too familiar scent of two day old sweat, camouflaged in cheap scent as he rambled on about Thursday nights being his night for catching up at the gym, yet showing no particular impressive signs in the abs. department. I quickly made my excuse to go to the ladies. As I walked across to the toilets, feeling slightly nauseated with the guy's bad odour, I was convinced that the only time I wanted to hear about catchments of muscle stimulating, adrenalin pumping workout sessions was from the girls, with our score cards at the ready as we admired from afar the array of bodies that really did impress us.

Whilst I was in the ladies powdering my nose, Anne was busy filling Stacey's head with the latest gossip, namely her shopping trip with James.

"Then he said, what about a book!"

"No, tell me he didn't"

"Yeah, so I dragged him into the knicker shop. Boy that was fun. By the time I'd finished with him he would of agreed to buy anything, just to get out of there!" she smiled over her glass at Stacey and nodded at her in confirmation to her statement.

"Serves him right. You'd think he'd know what to get her by now." replied Stacey and shook her head at the thought. "A book, Bloody hell!"

"Hey sis, where's the birthday girl gone?" asked Dave nudging at his sister's shoulder.

"Powder room, why"

"Just asking. Anyway where's her other half tonight"

"He's at the rugby!" chirped up Stacey, and sniggered into her glass.

"Are you tipsy already?" he continued, surprised at her silliness.

"No, just enjoying myself"

She looked over at Anne, who was by now chatting to one of her brother's friends and laughing. Dave smiled at Stacey and turned to answer a question from his friend, who was leaning over his shoulder to catch his attention. He took a swig from his pint, sauntered over to his friend's side and winked back at Stacey. Stacey felt sure she was going to blush and looked away, pretending not to have noticed.

"Hey, I didn't tell you did I?" continued Anne, turning back to finish her conversation with Stacey. "After he'd gone, I went back into the knicker shop and bought that bra!"

"Trust you. No prizes for guessing what you'll be getting up to"

"No prizes for guessing what Richard's going to be taking off." Anne chuckled and they started to laugh at the ridiculousness of their silly conversation.

On my return I spied one of my work colleagues, I think his name was Mark but I wasn't really sure, because of the high turn around in our office I didn't pay too much attention to the new ones any more as much as I should of. Anyway I noticed he was enjoying a drink with some of the lads from the office and started to chat to him in light hearted tones and raised the subject of rugby. After all most men liked to discuss some form of sport. And this would show him that I was more than capable of raising the resemblance of an intelligent conversation. He nodded with enthusiasm, approving of my choice of topics, so I decided to mention that James had gone to see the game.

"So where's the sanctimonious prick gone then?" he asked sniggering, swigging his third pint of lager for the night.

"Edinburgh" I replied ignoring his remark and then I thought 'I'll have to remember that line'

"Who's playing then?" I shrugged my shoulders and thought for a couple of seconds and then I remembered. But rather than tell him I decided it would be fun to make him figure it out for himself.

"Guess! Watch this"

I started to do my own version of the New Zealand rugby team dance with bent knees and outstretched tongue, projecting as far from my mouth as I could reach, my eyes making deliberate penetrating glares in sharp side to side motions.

"Huwala, Huwala" I chanted in the most ridiculous deepened voice I could channel "Hawa, Hawa"

Everyone started to laugh and chant the words "Yeah, The All Blacks!"

I mimicked slapping my hands down across the front of my legs, returning them to a waving signal followed by another:

"Huwa Lawa, Huwa Lawa, Lawa, lawa".

After two glasses of wine this was as far as I could muster but was pleasantly surprised to see the men had joined in with a chorus unbeknown to me and rattled off their own version to this ultimately famous rugby dance. After a few minutes of their entertaining display of skills we all gave ourselves a rapturous round of applause and at the same time we were holding onto to our stomachs from laughing so much.

My handbag was ringing a tune into my ear from the inside pocket. I quickly retrieved the phone to hear James's voice at the other end.

"Hi James"

"What a fantastic game Tess" He started "How's your birthday been…. hope you're not enjoying yourself too much without me pet?"

He had already wished me a happy birthday on the phone earlier this morning so he knew exactly what I was getting up to.

"Of course not, I miss you ……. James, I can hardly hear you over the noise"

"I said they won!" he shouted down the phone.

As I strained to listen James continued to tell me his account of the events and to my horror it turned out that it was the Africans playing against Scotland and not, as I had anticipated, the New Zealanders that day; and worse, the Africans had won the match.

"Oh, that's great" I uttered, feeling completely stupid at the blunder I'd just made.

"See you tomorrow, Love you!"

"Yeah, love you too" I replied and as I placed the phone back into my handbag it dawned on me just what had taken place minutes earlier.

Looking over towards the men I could see they were still laughing and swigging on their pints.

'Oh shit!' I thought, not again. Why was it I always made a complete fool of myself and worse, why did I always, always, always do it in front of the men? In the vane hope that they were going to consume so much alcohol that it would be impossible for them to remember anything of tonight's performance and maybe even be void of the knowledge that in reality it was the Africans playing, I decided to discreetly sneak off, back to where the girls were sitting.

Amazingly, the girls had been oblivious to my dancing skills and had been entertaining squirt's mates with their brilliant banter on their usual all time favourite topic of conversations, their latest trip to Majorca. Needless to say the sneak peaks of left over tans were still visible, especially when Stacey took it upon herself to pull her skirt down just enough to display an impressively tanned belly button, for her keen male onlookers to admire.

"I didn't know you had a belly button" teased Dave, admiring Stacey's new tan.

Stacey started to blush and tried to hide her embarrassment with her glass.

"Come on you two, we're supposed to be celebrating Tess's birthday" started Anne as she leapt to her feet "Let's check out the talent upstairs!"

Collecting our glasses we set off for a wander, to do some talent spotting. We ventured back up the main staircase to continue the rest of our evening with some new arrivals, who were heading towards the bar. Anne being the best chatter box in town, made the introductions for all of us. The drinks were inevitable after that. One gent after another would oblige us with a Bacardi or something; with a birthday kiss thrown in.

We took our places in one of the cubicles upstairs, which were much more flamboyant and spacious and accommodated better lighting for business men to finish their talks.

Birthday blessings of at least six or seven and a couple of hours later, we sidled our way back down the spiralling staircase and off into the ladies toilets. As Stacey perched herself behind the toilet door, she called out in an unmistakable drunken fashion.

"Where are you off to then?"

"London, not sure where in London though"

"All right for some, eh?"

I'd already filled the girls heads with my news about the London trip, whilst enjoying the gentlemen's drinks earlier and had told them that all about the new client I was soon to meet.

"Is he married?" Anne asked, determined to be brought up to date with the latest gossip.

"Nope, don't think so"

Anne and I positioned ourselves in front of the mirror, salvaging our lip lines and bashing our cheeks with even more camouflage from our refilled powder brushes.

Anne started to tell me of her account of a London trip she'd had.

"I ended up visiting some famous monument or other" she started "There was definitely chemistry between us, I'm telling you!"

It turned out this was yet another triumph for her when it came to choosing an inappropriate site for snogging. Knowing fine well that I didn't have a clue where anywhere was in London, she continued to taunt me.

"Well you just have to try out the new range at Harrods" Anne continued "You should see the collection of goodies I bought when I went there. Oh and you'll have to check out.......oh what's it called" Anne stopped to think for a moment, but she was interrupted by Stacey.

"I've been to a show there"

"Which one?" I asked

"Cats!.......it was brilliant. I stayed in this big hotel and everything!"

Stacey lined up next to us and studied her facial distortions, to assess the damage in the mirror. It felt that I had actually managed to live quite a sheltered life,

compared to the many expeditions my friends had been on.

We ventured out into the main corridor and leaned against a pillar quite close to the DJ stand, to watch the dancing. Before long we were taking steps towards the dance floor. Stacey and I giggled and pranced along, posing our usual flirtatious dance moves quite oblivious to everyone else around us. We took great pleasure in pretending to mime to the words of each song and over exaggerated our drama skills on all the high notes. Then a change of music forced us to recreate our own version of the wonderful ballad at the front of the Titanic, just before the ship was going down. Anne prompted us to replay the sinking part, so down we went as Anne pretended to snap the final photo shoot of us.

The end of a brilliant evening was drawing to a close and we sat the last one out. At least I was safe from James's reprisals this time. I was satisfied in thinking what a relief it was that I hadn't made a complete fool of myself in front of him this time!

Chapter nine

I find myself in a huge dilemma, pondering over the penultimate of all sacrifices every woman has to eventually endure in order to please her man. Retail therapy in essence is an art form that has to be nurtured and thought out, with true precision; to enable all women to show their men how to appreciate them and in return how to cherish his beloved female partner. Without her looks what is a woman to a man anyway, but some ordinary insignificant female blending in with the rest of society. Without retail extravagances no woman can truly look her best.

James had sprung an invitation on me that had come into his possession that read:

THE BLACK AND WHITE BALL
Charity Auction
To be held at: Belvedere Hall
On: November 15th
Invitation only
Dress code Black tie   Carriages 1.00 a.m.

I couldn't imagine what on earth I was going to wear. Knowing that I couldn't possibly fail him now I reached into my purse and retrieved the already well used credit card and checked the limit that I could spend. It was so typical of James to drop a bombshell like this on to my lap and I knew he would have no idea just how much it was going to cost me to dress for such an occasional. For a function as grand as this the price of a new dress was going to take me right up to my credit limit. And I figured he wouldn't offer to pay off my card at the end of the month, even though he knew full well that he earned more than I did; and the dress was going to be for him in the first place. Nevertheless this would have to be considered as a compulsory transaction in the making.

Whilst I was trying to figure out what kind of dress I was going to buy the men at the front of the office were busying themselves in the latest gossip.

"Yeah that's a really good one, send that" said Mark, giggling over some pictures of our rugby dancing skills, from Saturday night.

"Wait, she's at her desk now.......let's see if she notices"

"We could get this one blown up....... to a poster size" replied Mark, pointing to another one.

"Definitely. We could stick it behind the door of the gents then couldn't we!" another one cackled, to which everyone started to laugh.

Sat at my office desk with my justification in tact and objectively calculated, I quickly glimpsed down the emails in front of me. I knew I had escaped the obvious rituals of teasing from the men in the office as no one had even mentioned the obvious lack of knowledge on my part, when it came to Saturday's rugby. Which was a relief, as the men normally took great pleasure in tormenting me.

"Hey Tess..........?" shouted Mark "Have you recovered yet?"

"Yes thanks!" I confirmed and obligingly smiled back at him.

I continued to peruse the emails and noticed one unopened. And there it was proof, I hadn't escaped. Unbeknown to me somebody had photographed my attempts on their mobile phone. As I was dancing with my tongue still protruding out from my mouth they had taken the shot; and to embarrass me further decided to post it to me and probably everyone else in the bargain! I looked across to the men and realised I had just become the butt of their joke and worse, they knew I'd seen their email.

"How does it go again?....Tee hee. Laters!" said Mark laughing and promptly sat back down in his seat.

Yes, it had definitely been sent by one of the men in the office, but which one? I decided to vacate the premises as discreetly as possible and slipped away to consider my options in the retail therapy department.

After two hours pacing the streets, gathering nothing more than blisters for my troubles, I found myself on one of the main roads where I knew a huge department store would be. All I had to do was practice my cleverly devised art of snooping, long enough to sniff out a real bargain. It was just typical that it would have to be the wrong time of year for buying posh dresses and those all important retail sales wouldn't of started yet.

Trying on a black short dress then another, then another I finally stepped out of the changing room with what had to be the buy of the century. In the finest of black slinkiest fabrics and bathed in torrents of feathered lace, reaching down to the floor from the knees and trailing off behind me, I smiled with sheer pleasure in my heart. Yes! This time James was going to be so proud of me.

As I gazed into the tall mirror just in front of the rich pickings of accessories I could hear the upturned beat of a favourite song ringing out from the tall speakers. I did what any feather brained blonde would do and tested out the usefulness of this desirable gown to its full potential. As I wiggled my bottom and shimmied my hips to the music I could see in the mirror, from all the relevant angles, that this dress wouldn't be leaving anything to the imagination. Potentially this dress could reveal any unsightly VPL and only a good dose of lipo-suction through the old vacuum cleaner could do justice to my stomach now. On further inspection I saw staring back at me the 36C's with permanently erect nipples that no man could help but notice and no dress could disguise, without careful padding attached.

Unbeknown to me, sitting patiently at the front of the shop, a gentleman had been thoroughly entertained with my dancing skills and sidled over to where I was still posing the latest of many poses in front of the mirror. He casually walked over and leaned towards my right ear and whispered some well chosen words.

"If my wife could dance like that" he mused "with a figure like yours, I'd be buying that dress!"

"Oh……..do you think, thanks!" I replied optimistically and with that he smiled and sat back down, to wait for his wife's final choice of must haves for her wardrobe. Well I just had to buy the dress then. The reflection in the mirror started smirking triumphantly and I was convinced that things like that didn't happen very often. All I had to do now was build into the budget a rescue plan to mask my nipples, with the all important lingerie. As I waited to pay for my new dress the man's wife stepped out of the changing rooms to show him her taste in clothes.

I really felt for him as she had chosen a dress that did absolutely nothing for her figure, but she still persisted in asking him what he thought. He offered her an obligatory *you look very nice dear* and I couldn't help but smile, thinking how much more attention he had shown me when it came to choosing my dress, than he was showing his wife. As white lies are often compulsory in any marital situation, if people are supposed to save their face in such a crisis, he sounded pretty convincing to me.

As I continued to pace the streets, peering through an array of well dressed windows, I spotted the latest in strapless silicones dressing the female torso dummies, erected on blackened posts. La Senza had triumphed yet again in the art of enhancing a woman's breasts and even better came in various skin shades, to accommodate that sun tan you're going to get round to. I opted for the appropriate shade and dragged the matching g-string from its hook and joined the extended queue to display my well worn credit card.

With my successful purchases firmly positioned in the grasp of my hand, I set off home to way up how I was going to jazz up the rest of my outfit. There had to be at least one pair of black shoes in my never ending collection of boxed up bargains. Every time I had to choose between two or more pairs of shoes I always ended up convincing myself that if I buy them both, then one day the other pair will certainly come in useful. As I admired some beautiful jewellery pieces in yet another window, knowing it was going to become the all important accessory of all to finish off the look, I knew that nothing was going to compete with my very own wonderful bling collection back home. This was one area I definitely had in the bag.

One thing that is always missing when you find yourself shopping on your own is the companionship of a friend. And the lack of enthusiasm towards your latest buy becomes a lonely mission. By the time I'd managed to clear off any credit that was left on my credit card I was ready to call upon my dear friend Anne, knowing that she would be going to the ball too.

"Hi darling!" Anne greeted as she flung open the front door to her house.

"I couldn't help myself, I just had to buy this" I replied and rushed over to her couch dropping my bags down as I went and proceeded to pull out my new dress.

"Ouch, you're such a bitch!"

"What do you think?" I quizzed, beaming with excitement "Do you think James will like it?"

"Who cares what James thinks, go girl!" she replied approvingly. "Coffee?"

"Oooh yes please!"

I plonked down, next to my bags and cleared the clutter on to her floor. She had a very glamorous house, chrome fittings everywhere and white washed walls, plush with modern art. Everything about Anne's house portrayed her perfectly, from her designer coffee table to her array of Habitat style furnishings. Compact and bijou she called it and the kitchen was just the same. White tiles, units and crockery all decked off with blackened worktops and chrome fittings.

"You just have to see this, then girl" Anne said, placing two mugs of coffee on to the coffee table.

And she fetched her latest in over exaggerated bling, to reveal a fabulous pearl and crystal clustered bracelet.

"Oooooooh……..I love it" I said, really impressed.

"Look I'm glad I've seen you……." Anne started and plonked herself down next to me "Richard has asked me something and I don't know what to give him for an answer"

I couldn't help feeling a little bit confused by her revelation but pushed her to tell me more.

"Go on"

"He's asked me to ……..you know?"

"Oh yes. I'm so excited for you, tell him yes!……….Oh I absolutely love it!…..I'm so happy for you!" I answered instantly, thinking this was going to be her big moment.

"No you idiot, not that" Anne shrugged her shoulders, totally unimpressed with my reaction "He's asked me to spend Christmas with his family"

"Oh, is that all?"

"How do I tell him I can't go......well what I mean is I don't want to go. Anyway..... without hurting his feelings?"

"Since when did you ever care about anyone's feelings?" Anne slapped me on the arm and I just sat back and laughed at her lack of humour "No, just kidding!"

As we pondered over her dilemma we sat back and enjoyed our coffees together, relaxing into our typical friendly banter.

Chapter ten

The night of the Black & White Charity Ball was upon us. A taxi was waiting outside and James was ushering me to hurry up as I fussed over my usual last minute adjustments. He couldn't help acknowledging me with an enchanting smile of approval, to show that I had managed to buy the most successful of all dresses. I could see in the expression on his face that I had managed to please him in a way that makes him proud to have me hanging from his arm. I topped my outfit off with a white Gucci handbag edged in black; with one last check in the mirror I was ready to go.

On our arrival I promptly caressed his waiting friends and then I stepped back with my usual cheeky smile. We passed by an old wooden staircase, crossed over to some double doors at the other side of the hall and walked into a wonderful banquet hall. I started to admire the display of black and white table settings and chairs decorated in black and white fabrics, darning huge bows drawn into the backs. We collected our first complimentary glass of wine for the evening and mingled with the other guests. Concentrating on every detail of each conversation with a nod, I couldn't help tossing my hair back and tilting my head sideways to get a better view of my competition.

Tonight was going to be packed with lots of fun simply because I was in amongst friends, that I had grown to know over a number of years. Under normal circumstance I could guarantee that I would end up making a fool of myself, certainly after a few too many drinks, but when it came to being amongst friends I felt the excitement of knowing that no matter what I did tonight, nothing could possibly go wrong. Anne was going to be here soon with her partner Richard and the usual crowd from James's office had already started to arrive.

Sipping my first glass of wine I sensed a strong aroma of perfume wafting into the room and felt a hand come round my waist. Sure enough it was Anne's.

"Hi darling"

"Oh, you look lovely" I replied, impressed with her choice in dress.

Anne had chosen a fabulous black cocktail dress, covered in sequins and was wearing long white gloves. She'd topped it off in her usual style with the most amazing chunky, diamante bracelet.

"Hi Richard" I greeted as he plonked a charming kiss to my hairline.

"Looking ravishing as ever Tess" and gently placed his hand on my shoulder.

Richard was about 5'11" tall and even though he wasn't as slim lined as James, he hid a dashing figure beneath his clothes.

Anne proceeded to slap a whopper on James cheek in bright plum shaded lipstick.

"Hey you" James replied and proceeded to shake Richard's hand.

Anne brushed up against my shoulder to admire her handiwork still evident on poor James's face. Giggling at the impression Anne had just left on James, I decided not to tell him.

"Hey Tess........?" started Richard "Tell us again what you want for Christmas this year?"

In a previous conversation, lead by my total confusion and lack of knowledge on the topic of cars, I had pointed out my love for a certain one in particular.

"A Lambughatti" I laughed and Anne quickly warned her boyfriend in a soft voice, knowing what was coming next.

"Leave her alone Rick!"

"No seriously......." he continued, chuckling. "Is it a cross breed then.........or is what you get when a Bugatti has a leg over with a Lamborghini?...... Did they tell Jeremy Clarkson about this one?"

I raised my hand to cover my somewhat red face in embarrassment. Still laughing at Richard's choice of words I couldn't resist the temptation to snort into my glass, spraying the back of James's jacket with the wine, which brought on even more giggles from my friends. Suddenly I felt a gentle squeeze from Richard, to show he was only teasing me.

Anne and I disappeared off to the powder room to do our usual checks in the mirror, while the men got to work on catching up on the latest gossip.

"So James, did you hear about Tess's cock up, the other week?" Richard asked.

"What's she been up to this time?"

"Well, you know you went to see Africa verses Scotland?"

"Yeah……..?"

"She only paraded about the night club doing a rendition of the All Blacks"

"Nothing surprises me with that one" James cringed at the notion and started to smirk.

"Listen, we've got an email of it, I'll send it to you" confirmed Richard, sniggering.

Anne and I reassembled our hairstyles to remove the evidence of our windswept journey, then onto the all important reapplication of makeup. I hitched up the front of my dress and started to tell Anne about my new purchase in the latest of bras.

"It's made from some kind of special foam or wadding" I started "You've got to be careful though, 'cause if you push your nail or something into it, it leaves a dimpled impression." by this time Anne had turned to admire the new bust line I had invented in my new dress.

"Suits you" she confirmed, somewhat dismissively and continued to apply her makeup.

"They told me you can't wash it and you have to lay it down flat in your drawer" I continued.

"So you mean to tell me, I have to find a drawer 38 inches wide and double D's deep. Yeah right" Anne replied in sniggering tones and she hitched her bust up at the reflection in the mirror, as if to emphasise her cup size.

"Can you imagine then……." she continued with humorous intent "If you could buy your knickers in the same stuff?"

"What do you mean?"

"Well you wouldn't exactly be able to wash your knickers, now would you?" she replied, showing her usual warped sense of humour.

"Oooooooh……… trust you" I said cringing at the thought.

"Just think, they could promote their own brand of dimple enhancing knickers. You know…." Anne continued in overtones of well executed pretentiousness "To enhance one's bottom! To match the dimples nature gave us in the first place!"

We both started wagging our bottoms at each others reflections in the mirror and with that we both bellowed in over exerted laughter. I just knew we were definitely on our way to a good night out with these lines!'

"Do you know what I think they should make?"

"I dread to think!" I replied, waiting for yet another sarcastic one liner.

"Cup sized knickers……..you know for women who want bigger bottoms!"

"You are so sick girl!"

"Yeah I know, but it wouldn't work anyway would it?"

"This is going to be really bad…..I just know it"

"If they opted for double of any size, it wouldn't do them any favours" Anne continued, contorting her bottom to a sitting position "'Cause look….as soon as you sit down they'd become deflated!"

"Sick……..and definitely warped!" I laughed as Anne emphasised her perfectly formed posterior.

Just behind us some women had started up a conversation, which was to ultimately ridicule one of the guests in her bad taste in clothes. They were queuing for a cubicle to become vacant and they seemed be cackling in a cruel choice of words. All we could make out was that they were mocking this guest's choice of dress and as the conversation progressed they began to mock the size of the woman's back. I imagined this huge woman with ripples of fat, pouring over a giant rusted safety pin.

And sure enough the woman in question walked in. She was wearing a long white evening gown and it definitely wasn't wide enough to fasten across the width of her large back. She nagged her friend to do something with the fastenings on her dress to recover her dignity, emphasising the fact that it had pulled away. The gossiping women looked on still sniggering. We sneaked a glimpse very discreetly through the mirror and peered over at the unmistakable down sized gown in its true mess. By now her friend was trying to help, insisting the woman kept still so she could be hitched back into it with a safety pin. She looked thoroughly fed up with all the nagging she was receiving, so we just looked on in sympathy to her plight. It obviously wasn't her fault in the first place and she didn't seem to be getting any thanks for her efforts.

We quickly made our escape and exited the toilets, not wanting to get trapped in the heat of any argument. Anne and I couldn't help smirking at each other in amusement.

"Some people genuinely think that even if they pile the weight on, the dress will still fit" I said tutting at the woman's stupidity.

"Well, now she's just found out how wrong she is" replied Anne optimistically.

Everyone had now started to make their way over to the appropriate tables so we quickly resumed our places with the men and took our seats. Anne and I chose to sit together and she quickly busied herself in whispering into Richard's ear, as she pointed out the woman in the white dress to him. The woman was still looking extremely flustered, but fortunately she wasn't going to be sitting next to us.

"Do you remember Deborah and Simon?" said James, pointing out the couple next to him. "Deborah's one of our solicitors"

"Oh hi. Yes……I remember" I replied and smiled at their expectant faces.

The meal was the usual façade of courses indicative of this type of event, going completely unnoticed amidst the volumes of chatter and merriment. Everyone began talking louder and louder and some occasional exchanges of humour kept everyone in light hearted spirits. We waded through the starters then the main course, fitting in the occasional responses to the latest gossip as we ate.

"Can you pass me the wine mate?" Simon heckled in Richard's direction.

"Yeah sure, oh there's only red left" he replied, tipping an empty bottle as evidence.

"I'm stuffed, aren't you?" I asked leaning over to Anne.

"Well I'm still peckish"

"Then onto the piggishly delicious desserts we shall go!" I replied grinning at her response.

By the time we had settled down to our coffees the usual speeches were under way. The extended thanks to the magician who had just spent the evening entertaining the audiences, showing off his latest card tricks as he worked the floor from one table to the next. Then the commentator continued to rave on about the talented voice of our guest singer who had taken it upon himself to sing into some poor unsuspecting lady's ear, earlier in the evening. Then a round of applause rang out for him in acknowledgement of a job well done.

"Are you alright, sweetheart?" asked James, placing his hand on my knee and kissed me gently on my cheek.

I beamed back at him and nodded in agreement, knowing fine well I was more than alright. He'd spent a lengthy time chatting to Deborah next to him, about something or other to do with work and had inadvertently left me out of the proceedings. But this time I wasn't bothered as I had the trusted company of my dear friend Anne to entertain me.

"Of course, what was all that about?"

"Deborah's got a court hearing on Monday. She's a bit anxious that's all"

"Anne thinks she's seen her somewhere before"

"Probably, she's always involved in litigation. Anne's place will use her a lot I should imagine" he confirmed

Well, what ever that meant it certainly sounded impressive, but not wanting to look too stupid I decided to keep quiet and not mention it again. I sat round to face the main speaker and nudged my way back onto James's leg as I listened.

The commencement of the evening's auction extravaganza had just started and in amongst all this gaiety the auction pieces were one by one being sold off. The occasional nudges to partners were taking place across the tables as people sought to scoop yet another bargain. We settled down to coffee and mints as we watched the silliness of the auction prizes. Anne had tried to coax poor Richard into buying her a man servant for a day. Surprisingly enough he declined much to everyone's amusement, but not Anne's!

The music had got under way and people were doing there usual shuffling to the beat. Not wanting to miss out on the dancing I set off with the girls to burn off some calories to the music. We chatted away oblivious to the rest of the dancers around us, still hitting the right beat with our titivating moves. Before long James and Richard had joined us and we pretended to perform our own style of come dancing. In actual fact James could do this far better than I ever could, he strutted his stuff with his stylish moves while Richard enchanted us all with his word perfect choruses to the usual choice of music. We cruised the floor, dipped and turned, doing the usual crashing into people as we carouselled the floor space, encouraging the other men to join us. And before long the minutes had turned to hours without a gap in the middle.

I started to cross the room stopping just long enough next to our table to take another swig of wine and headed off towards the toilets. Anne was heading straight for me and suddenly she grabbed me by the arm.

"Come on, it's started already" she shrieked, obviously in good spirits.

"Hang on!" I said as she dragged me back towards the dance floor but Anne was in a rush to get things moving.

"This is one of my favourite party pieces!" she shrieked.

"Okay, okay......I get it already" and I quickly followed on behind; dragging bodies of people to join us as we went.

As tipsy as I was, I carefully hitched up my skirt just enough for James to sit down in front of me. We clambered on to the floor dragging our partners down between our outstretched legs. We ended up with at least three rows of giggling bodies already to do the next party dance, reminiscent of all good do's. Beating the floor with our hands, first on one side then over to next side, we chanted a chorus.

"Hoops up side yer head, I said hoops up side yer head. Hear we go!"

We all frantically started to perform our rowing skills. The more we pushed each other forwards and backwards, then side to side, we chanted this ridiculously funny song.

Laughing so much it suddenly dawned on me why I had left the dance floor in the first place. Even worse I was no longer able to do anything about it as the rowing song was still going strong. When you're legs are in this position I can say with some confidence, that ultimately you cannot stop yourself from having a pee!

As the dance came to an end James picked himself up from the floor and reached out his hand to pull me up. Fortunately as I pulled the contours of my dress back down, I noticed the tiny accident which had taken place was hidden between the layers of the feathery lace. I could just about save my face for the night. The slow dances had started to play signalling that the end of the night was upon us as James firmly placed his arm around my waist. This was an encounter I wasn't going to forget in a hurry. We circled the dance floor in slow motion as gracefully as we could. First one song, then another and every now and again we kissed each other, as I snuggled up into James's neck for the rest of the night.

Chapter eleven

s we walked back into my apartment I was still searching my brain
for the latest rendition to my journal. James closed the door behind
me as I wandered off into the living room to think. And then it struck me:
*'Love is: smooching with your boyfriend on the dance floor in a beautiful soiled
gown'* I thought and sneaked off into the bedroom to write it down, while
I could still remember it.

"I'll stick the kettle on then, shall I?" James teased as I disappeared.

James took it upon himself to create the perfect sobering tonic by
preparing some mugs of coffee for our late night drink. Whilst he waited
for the kettle to boil, he went back to the living room to take off his jacket.
I watched intently from the bedroom doorway as he started positioning
his jacket in folds across the back of the settee in his usual typical style and
I stood there romanticising over all the wonderful, exciting memories of
our night out.

"Are you still with us?" James turned to render me a warming smile and
returned to the kitchen, to resume his duty of coffee making.

"Hmm…….." I offered wandering off into a world of my own and
made a ditched attempt at smiling.

I had other ideas for the evening's finale and it definitely did not include
coffee! So I made the decision to follow James back into the kitchen. Slowly
I crept up to him and squeezed my finger tips into his ribs.

"Stop it silly" he laughed, still trying to spoon out the coffee into the percolator.

"Who wants coffee at a time like this" I asked snuggling up to his back.

"You're drunk Tess" he said in gentle tones as he pursued his mission.

But I was having none of it and started to pull him back away from the worktop.

"Tess.......stop it sweetheart" he laughed and stopped what he was doing to face me.

He wrapped his arms around my waist and offered me a loving kiss, to pacify my silly behaviour.

Coaxing him with my hands tugging at his waist, I lured him out of the kitchen and over to the bedroom door. He started grinning and went along with my playfulness as I gently persuaded him into the bedroom, by holding his hands and walking in backwards.

"Come into my boudoir, darling"

"Very funny" he laughed still holding my hands and watched me, intrigued as to my intentions.

I placed him into position, turning his back towards the end of the bed and in a teasing gesture, I pushed him down into a sitting position at the edge of the bed. I leaned over to kiss his forehead and nudged his legs together with my legs either side of his. By this time James was becoming very receptive towards me and from this point on he just couldn't help himself. The smile on his face went from a slightly puzzled expression to a full toothed smile of expectant satisfaction.

"I love you when you're like this"

"Really, how much?" I joked, messing up his hair.

I continued to tease him as I sat on his lap with my knees firmly placed either side of his body in a kneeling pose. I loosened the zip on my dress and carefully pealed off the top part to reveal my newly enhanced cup size.

"Do you like?" I teased pushing my breasts towards his face.

"Oh yes……….!" he replied convincingly "You looked gorgeous tonight!"

Pushing him slightly back I revealed my real contours, by removing the incriminating bra.

"And now…?" I asked, still blatantly emphasising my cleavage.

"Especially……..now!"

At this stage I had to laugh at the pleasurable expression on his face and start bringing his hands in to assist me in my playful tormenting of his manly needs.

"Which one do you like the best……. this one?" I tormented him, pointing out one of my breasts.

James did what any good honest, decent boyfriend would do. He cupped each one in turn and resumed a considerate, thoughtful and carefully observational expression on his face, as he weighed up his options in front of him.

"Both!"

The only light showing in the bedroom was a gentle beam seeping in from the kitchen. For some reason it didn't even seem to matter, that I hadn't thought to close the curtains. All I knew was, if I stopped now the distraction would kill the moment. James pulled me down on top of him, still smiling and rolled me over as if to take charge of the situation. Positioning his strong arm beneath my body, James took hold of me and with a firm grip he repositioned me towards the head of the bed. With a kiss pressed into my breast, he pulled himself up and obligingly pulled away at his tie and loosened his top buttons on his shirt. He took the masculine of poses and revealed his chest by drawing his shirt up over his head. Tonight he definitely wasn't going to waste any time with the rest of the shirt fastenings. This would of taken far too long. With the shirt tossed to the floor he proceeded to finish removing my dress, raising me slightly by my waist and shifting my weight on to his arm, as the dress was peeled down my legs to join the crumpled shirt on the floor.

"Now……..where were we?" he teased.

"Oh, you'll figure it out" I replied, rolling my finger inwards in a gesturing motion.

By now James had started to tantalise my bodily pulses as he graced my neck with his kisses and gently he moved his lips towards my chest, caressing me with his motions. My whole body was tingling and responding very appreciatively to his tender touches. Down he went with each kiss landing in a new place; settling on my nipple then my rib cage down to my belly button. Further he went to the top of my bikini line, checking my responses as he went with warming strokes from his tender hands.

The last kiss placed, James pulled himself to his feet and moving towards the end of the bed he kicked off his shoes and dragged off his socks, scattering them across the floor. Then he stood tall and braised himself to unfasten his trousers. He removed them with a strong determined stance and stepped back towards the bedroom door. With one quick shove from his outstretched hand the door bolted itself shut, trapping any sign of light on the other side. In that one move James had set the mood for the rest of the night. Another chapter in our sexual relationship had just begun.

We weren't the only ones making tracks either. Anne was determined that it was going to be pay back time for poor Richard, after refusing to bid for a man servant for her. She took him back to her kitchen to show him the repercussions of his actions.

"So, you think it was funny to lose me a man servant do you?"

"What?" Richard asked rather bewildered.

Anne turned him to face her and pulled him into the kitchen, buffing him up against the worktop.

"Now, this is what I want you to do" Anne started with delicious intent. "I want you to clean up everything on my worktop. And I mean everything!"

Richard knew all to well what Anne was up to and quickly moved in on her. He embraced her with a confirmative kiss and picked her up, plonking her on top of the worktop.

"Very well, if you insist"

"Oh bad boy" she teased as Richard made headway of removing her shoes.

"And you, are a very bad girl"

But Anne was determined to have much more fun out of him and leaned over to where the pinny was hanging.

"Oh no, Richard. You won't be getting off that easy. You have some serious cleaning up to do!" she continued and shoved the offending pinny in his face.

Richard looked staggered for a moment and held it out in dismay.

"What on earth?"

"Well you have to look the part. How else can I be sure you're the man for the job!" Anne had full intentions of dressing him down, not up and pointed in the direction of the bedroom, for him to go and change into his new uniform. He chuckled, knowing he had just been set up and obligingly strolled off to the bedroom.

Whilst Richard was busy removing his clothes, Anne set to work on removing some of hers. She peeled off her dress leaving just the essential lingerie and gloves, still darning the chunky bracelet. She poured out two glasses of wine and repositioned herself across the worktop to torment him further.

Richard stepped out wearing just his uniform, the pinny and smiled intensely on seeing his new chore for the evening. Laid out across the work surface holding out a glass of wine, Anne had posed her most glamorous of poses for him.

"And I intend you to make a very thorough job of it Richard" Anne chanted with authority and deliberately started to spill some wine down her front.

"Whoops!" she taunted "This first I believe!"

Richard was revelling in the prospect of assisting his naughty wench and moved in on his task at hand. In no time at all Richard was making good headway of the situation, much to Anne's delight!

Chapter twelve

Zigzagging across the city via a tube station, not really sure of where I was going, I was desperately searching for the hotel I was going to be staying at. The trip to London had finally arrived and I had no time to lose before meeting my prospective client.

I had taken the 8.15 a.m. train and headed off towards London. With my map at the ready and the hand written messages of directions, which I had received from the boss's secretary, I finally arrived at the hotel. Straight in front of me was the most enormous set of doors and I was pleasantly greeted by a couple of very polite door men who assisted me with my baggage. I quickly checked in with less than an hour left to spare before my big meeting.

Gathering up my holdall, files and handbag I quickly headed towards the lift that had just arrived. Three men were already waiting in the lift, staring towards me as I rummaged through my handbag and I politely requested the third floor button to be depressed. The tallest dark haired stranger to the back of me I couldn't see, but he stayed silent and uninterested in any of the conversations taking place in the lift. The shorter European looking gent was chatting away, showing obvious signs that he worked out in the gym. You know the kind. His trousers were firmly wrapping themselves around his rather firm thighs. I couldn't help but realise that I was paying far too much attention to this remarkable phenomena.

The third man looked rather straggly, medium height but not very distinguished at all; with rather plain dusty looking shoes, that had passed their sell by date a long time ago. He started up a conversation with me that clearly was to amuse him and the others present, but was going to bore the hell out of me.

"So where are you from love?" He asked in a very broad accent and I suddenly realised he looked just like a doorman.

By this time I had the most horrendous headache kicking in. After all, I'd just travelled the length of the country for the past few hours without as much as a bite to eat all day. This was going to be the headache that would potentially ruin my whole afternoon if I didn't find some heachache pills soon. So I replied with indifference to the man's lack of tact and diplomacy.

"Lancashire"

"What brings you to London then eh, love?" he continued with the same blunt egotistical banter.

"A train!" I delivered an equally blunt reply with an increased tone of disdain. That was twice now he'd had the cheek to call me *love* and I really hated that personable use of the word.

"Would you mind?" I continued "Only I have a really bad headache"

"So what've you been doing to get yerself a headache then, eh?" he persisted in total ignorance of my intolerance towards him.

I sighed impatiently at this point as I had no intentions of amusing him for much longer. I decided to knock the smug smirk from his quite gaunt face by attacking him with the full force of my usual charm, when I take a disliking to somebody.

"I do not appreciate having to talk to a man who cannot be bothered to clean his shoes in the morning. What concern it could be of yours, as to what I have been doing, I can't imagine!" I started, in an irritated manner "I assure you; you would not be a suitable substitute to join in at any level!"

Yes, I had actually lowered my standards to insulting men in lifts. Oh well, I did say I had a headache.

His disgruntled tones were reaching my ears even more now as he allowed the indignation to arouse his curiosity. His reply to my unpleasant reprisal became compulsory by nature; and yet again in a serious and still blunt snigger, he continued to taunt me with further drivel.

"I'll have you know love; that I happen to work for a very important company... And the boss definitely doesn't like mouthy women like you".

The insult slapped me in the face with such a force, he had actually lowered his standards to the gutter level and this would not relieve me of my obligations to reply either.

"Leave her alone" whispered the European chap clearly disapproving of his friend's remark She's already told you she has a headache, hasn't she?"

But no headache was going to allow me to be humiliated in this way despite my remarking on his shoes. What right had he to remark on me as a person? Vengeance was soon to arrive with wicked tenacity. The lift door opened at the third floor stop so I gracefully wedged my foot in the path of the door, long enough to resume communications with this individual. I turned and faced this argumentative man, smiled sarcastically and sweetly chanted my retaliation.

"Are you a gambling man?" I quipped. Without waiting for a reply I continued "Do you have a tenner on you?"

Slightly confused with my response to his insult, he rose to the bait.

"Yeah I have love, here" and he reached for his wallet and produced one lonely ten pound note and waved it at me.

I turned towards his colleague who had graciously defended me. I couldn't help but notice; he had an amazing olive complexion and a rather distinctive roman nose. And with a much softer and pleasant tone in my voice, I asked:

"Have you ever met me before?"

"No" he said with a very puzzled look on his face.

"Good" and I immediately turned back to face his associate, to dish out the gamble the he could not win.

"If your friend here can tell me my name, you lose the tenner. But if he can't, you win and I will pay you. Agreed?"

With a frown of suspicion on his face, still puzzled by my challenge, he agreed. I turned back to his colleague and pointed discreetly up towards my file which I was holding. Moving my hand away from the front of the file, the man could see my name badge attached. In order to help me in my quest, by cheating his friend out of the money, smiling at what I had just done he suddenly told me my name.

"Tess Bannister"

"Correct!" I said grinning and turning to his assailant I held out my hand and he delivered his tenner into my palm, totally bemused and disappointed.

As I left the lift, I turned to face my new partner in crime.

"I believe this tenner is yours and thanks for that!" and as an after thought I continued "Perhaps you should teach your friend how to read!"

And with that I giggled a little and removed my foot from the doorway and smuggly made my escape down the corridor and off to my room.

The next twenty minutes I managed to resemble the look of someone slightly more presentable. With a quick change and tidy up of my appearance, I was ready to go back down to the foyer to meet my new client.

Chapter thirteen

I wasn't sure what to expect, all I knew was that I had this funny feeling in my stomach that I was going to re-sit my very first interview all over again. This meeting

was to promote my company and ultimately, just to please an important client. Straight ahead of me I could see two gentlemen sat talking and as I approached I noticed one of them was the European gent from the lift. He looked towards me and continued to speak some quiet words with his associate. I wasn't sure what to do, so I observed him for a second and felt sure that this other man was going be the one I had come to see.

I was right. As I looked around the foyer I couldn't help but notice, from the corner of my eye, the European gent just getting up to leave. He looked across at me and grinned then promptly gestured the other man to his feet. The second rose from his seat and looked across at me with a sensible, yet quite charming smile. As I extended my hand to his, I started to introduce myself.

"Good afternoon, I'm, Tess Bannister"

"It's alright, I know who you are" he said shaking my hand "Just call me Andy"

Confused, I smiled and tried to figure out how on earth he could have known who I was.

"Would you care to sit down?" He asked gesturing me to sit and join him at his table.

"Thanks" I replied and started to cleverly devise a way of placing my files in front of him, to which he quickly acknowledged and took his place at the table.

I found myself sitting in a very comfy carver chair relaxing back into the seat, making full use of the polished wooden arms.

"That was a neat trick you pulled, back in the lift" and suddenly the penny dropped. He must have been the other man, stood behind me back in the lift earlier this afternoon. I quickly remembered the words my boss had said to me: '*Don't mess this up!*'

"Oh, I'm sorry about that"

"It's alright," he continued with a gentle laugh of encouragement "It served him right for having a go at you. How's your headache now?"

"My head is still playing up" I told him unable to stop myself from smirking.

I continued to tell him all about the long journey I had taken to get here and my lack of ability to master the tube timetables.

"I suppose it's quite hard for you in unfamiliar territory" he assured me.

"Just a bit"

As he spoke, I couldn't help but notice that he had a more working class manner about him. He didn't have the airs and graces that James had distinguished himself in, but at the same time Andy seemed to have a much more relaxed manner about him, that was to become a refreshing change for the rest of day. In his appearance he resembled an entrepreneur of the highest making, with the latest in designer suits and the jazziest of cufflinks. He had darned a dark, open necked shirt, as opposed to the more traditional shirt and tie which I had grown to expect.

I couldn't help watching as he glanced down the pages of my portfolio, waiting for some tell tale sign of approval or other. Then he looked over his shoulder and hastened a member of staff over.

"Coffee?" He asked, turning to me as he gestured.

"Please"

"Yeah two coffees please, thanks!" and carried on reading.

I nodded and thought how on earth can you display such authority like that without any effort? The lack of conversation was making me nervous but not for long. He eventually turned to face me and resumed talking in pleasant basic tones, offering occasional enthusiastic remarks towards my company.

"So this is going to be for five years, yes?"

"That's right, but as you can see there's a sixty month finance option plan"

All in all it was going well. After answering his somewhat straight forward questions, I found myself settling down to the more informal approach Andy was showing towards me.

We drank our coffee and chatted for what must have been over half an hour, maybe more. It turned out the European gent was one of his colleagues and the other man in the lift did indeed work for him.

"The guy who upset you happens to be my driver"

"So he's not a doorman then?"

"What on earth made you think that?"

"I couldn't help but notice his mucky shoes. …Sorry"

"It's alright, no skin off my nose" he replied and continued to be amused by my observations.

Apparently, Andy had quietly observed the situation and drawn his own conclusions on the matter. I was glad it wasn't somebody too important. If it had of been I could of seriously jeopardised this whole meeting.

Andy clearly had a good reputation in the world of business. From what I had read about him, I had learnt that at quite a young age he had set up a software business followed by some kind of estate company. By the time he had reached twenty five he had sold his software business for a few million, yet still kept hold of a share holder's stake. From there he had generated a group of companies in media throughout Cheshire and London that stood him a hefty income. Affording me any of his time to meet with him, meant he had to rearrange his London trip to slot me in. In no time at all I sensed a strong air about him, not in an intimidating way but enough to feel that he was big and I was definitely small.

The meeting was being interrupted continuously by this time with a steady influx of people arriving in the foyer. They were already dumping clusters of luggage, close to our table and hogging the reception area to catch someone's attention. So Andy suggested that we retreat to a more civilised setting away from the crowds.

"Look, I'm sorry.......why don't we take this somewhere a little less noisy, shall we?" he asked rising from his seat.

"That's fine with me"

At this we walked across to the bar and peered through the entrance. But the bar was becoming decidedly crowded, with even more over zealous banter taking place.

This was the first time I had really paid much attention to him. Even though Andy was certainly taller than me, which wasn't too difficult really, he wasn't as tall as James. Andy seemed much broader and had a strong jaw line with a very stylish unshaven look about him. His hands were quite large and I couldn't help but notice his nails were not as professionally manicured as I would of expected. Nevertheless I felt incredibly honoured to be standing alongside him and had no objection whatsoever in him carrying my pile of documents for me. Suave and sophisticated would be how I would be describing him to my friends; and I would go as far as saying, he even smelt good enough to eat.

Andy paused for a moment and I sensed he was contemplating his next step. He obviously wanted to talk some more, but became quite irritated with the noise around us.

"Have you eaten yet?" He asked inquisitively.

"No. Not yet"

"The only way we can resume this meeting is for us to retire to our rooms" he said as he continued to figure something out in his head. "I tell you what.......I'll arrange a table for us in a restaurant"

"If you think that's best" I answered, feeling slightly excited over the prospect of going to dinner with him.

"Yes, we'll do that then. That way it will give me more time to way up my options"

I sensed he seemed genuinely concerned in the fact that I had taken the time out, to follow him the length and breadth of the country, to actually have this meeting so I nodded in agreement, thinking this was a good opportunity to have a break in my room and a free meal into the bargain,

"Okay"

"And I assure you, that I will be returning this later on" he said, waving my files at me in a promising gesture.

I'd had the good sense to bring a change of clothing with me. After all, if I was going to make this contract happen I had to prove ready and able, on his command. Andy was going to be escorting *me*, 'Miss Professional Bimbo 2009' to a posh restaurant. Now I could play lady muck for the night in shining armour, or just enjoy a well earned meal. Either way tonight was going to prove very interesting.

Chapter fourteen

s we arrived at the entrance to a most impressive restaurant I couldn't help but notice queues of people were forming, eagerly waiting to be seated. Andy took control of the situation and introduced himself to an expectant waiter. W hung around a while as he perused over the long list of wines on the wine menu. The corridor of crowds became deafeningly loud and the surging heat started to suffocate me. With my head still pounding I sensed that all was not well, each step becoming heavier as I tried to stay upstanding. I could see Andy standing just a few feet away in front of me. As he slowly turned round to face me I reached out my arm to him, trying desperately to tell him of my demise. I knew something was wrong and my mind started to play tricks on me. The curtains started to close in on me in swathes of blackened smoke, turning the people into drifts of swirling grey. My body simply folded beneath me as I passed out in front of him.

As the smog started to clear I sensed a light peering through the openings of my eyes. I began to visualise myself standing in what could only be described as a restaurant kitchen. The setting was all wrong and I wasn't convinced that I was even in the same restaurant anymore. There was laughter all around me and as I moved round the room I saw a huge griddle and a Greek waiter stood along side me, happily chomping into his pitta bread filled with meat balls and he was dunking it into some taramasalata dip. The door behind me flung open and a beautiful Greek dancer walked in, in bare feet. I closed my eyes for a second and then I looked again. This time I knew I had to be dreaming as she was still standing there, posing with a colourful sash and dangling her coins attached to her skirts. She seemed to jingle with each step she took, as she shimmered in her skimpy top. All of a sudden I was circling the waiter, with my fingers walking over his broad shoulder to the back of his neck and continued across to his other shoulder, until arriving in front of him. I don't know what it was about Greeks but in this dream he managed to have a sexual attraction about him. I looked on in disbelief as I seemed to be teasing him and caressing his hair with my fingers; whilst nibbling on his right ear lobe. In this peculiar world I had managed to tantalise and charm this waiter and concluded my pleasure in brushing up close to his body and whisper in his ear.

"I'll show you my dance, if you show me your bazooka!"

Then I noticed the dancer started to beckon me, pointing towards the hot griddle with a gesturing arm. Obligingly I started to flick my hips and bending backwards over the griddle I started to perform my own belly dance. I was laughing and booting my right hip up towards the ceiling in quick motions, as the waiter stood by, clapping in approval. As I reached out my arms I started to shake my shoulders to a steady beat, tipping my head back as I went. Even though there was no sound or than the constant laughter I could still feel the rhythm and the essence of sizzling hot kebabs from the griddle was reaching my nose.

Suddenly the waiter was coming towards me in a frantic rush, waving a glass of water in his outstretched hand. Sensing that my hair may be catching fire I felt the first signs of water trickling from my face, like a shower of rain drops.

"Can you hear me?" the voice kept calling to me from the distance, getting louder, louder, until… "Tess. Are you alright?"

I looked up and there was a familiar face shadowing my view. Andy was gently wiping my face with cubes of ice, embedded deep into a tea towel.

"Are you alright?" he repeated, smiling down at me.

Unable to speak, I slowly looked around and realised I was now in a large office, lying down on a couch that had been propped up against a white washed wall. A young waitress was stood by him.

"Shall I get more ice, sir?"

"No" Andy replied. "I think she'll be fine now".

"Are you alright........I was worried about you?" Andy started "You fainted right in front of me"

In his quest to carry me to safety he had called in the service of the restaurant manager who quickly came to our aid and had escorted us into his private office. Andy carefully tucked his hands under my arms and lifted me up, then he passed me a glass of iced cold water.

"Here, drink this" he said and I sipped obliging whilst Andy kept hold of the glass.

"Send for my car" he ushered the manager and he speedily left the room with his waitress trotting along behind.

"I'm sorry" I said feeling somewhat embarrassed.

"Don't worry" he replied in a sympathetic tone. "I knew something was wrong, you'd turned as white as a ghost."

I was still confused so decided to keep quiet for a while, observing Andy's careful handling of the situation. After a few minutes the door opened and in walked the manager.

"It's here sir" and propped the door open with his foot.

"Gently does it" Andy said as he helped me backed onto my feet.

I just managed a smile in response and allowed him to take my hand, to guide me back out of through the office door.

He continued guiding me back through the restaurant to the entrance doors. Still holding my hand, he ushered the driver to open the car door and once opened he took a side step, affording me enough room to get back into his car. Still feeling shaky I sat back into my seat, whilst Andy got in next to me from the other side.

"I am never going to travel on an empty stomach again" I whispered to him.

He offered me a gracious smile of encouragement and told the driver to take us back to the hotel. Tilting my throbbing head back, I decided to keep quiet for the rest of the journey all the way back to the hotel.

Chapter fifteen

There was already quite a bit of activity going on in the hotel foyer so Andy quickly guided me over to the lift. He was a quiet sort of man and I couldn't help noticing his calmness after everything that had happened. He generated a certain warmth and seemed to put me at my ease whilst in his presence.

"You still haven't eaten anything yet, have you?"

"No"

"I'm going to order some food up to my room and see if we can't track down any pills, for that head of yours!" he said.

Without really being sure of how to answer this, I realised he had declared a statement rather than a question. I looked at him not really knowing what I should do.

"Are you sure?"

"I am not letting you go back to your room on an empty stomach"

The lift came to a halt and I followed him out into the corridor. Immediately adjacent to the lift was a door with a brass name plate. It read 'Marquis Suite'. Andy positioned a card in the lock and ushered me in. As I followed behind a great sense of disbelief came over me. I quietly composed myself as I started to take a look at the décor surrounding me.

Everywhere I looked the room was draped in beautiful ivory fabrics. The curtains merged from the ceiling down to the floor and beyond in heavy wadded silken fabrics, with swags and tails framing the look. Andy stood back and watched as I admired the room. I polished the surface of the sideboard with the palm of my hand sensing the coldness of the top, which had lots of layers of lacquer applied to it, protecting the rich pickings of gold detail embedded into the top.

"You're easily impressed" he said, smiling at the impression on my face.

"Oh, it's lovely" I replied, still keeping a keen eye on the décor.

"Make yourself at home…" he said as he picked up the telephone "I'm going to phone down for some food, okay?"

"Okay" I answered only half paying attention.

The size of the grand bed was stunning as it sat on its very own platform, but I thought better of going over to it, just in case I gave Andy the wrong impression. So I just stared at the bedspread, which was trailing down to the floor in beautifully finished and heavily wadded quilted ivory fabric. As I turned round I took in every detail of the furnishings. Even the huge couch was complimenting the room in a plush embossed ivory fabric and huge cushions.

"Yes, and can we have some wine sent up as well………." said Andy, still keeping his eye on me as he continued to order our dinner from room service and smiled at me in amusement. "Oh, wait and can you find me some headache tablets. Thanks"

By this time I was busy stroking the back of his couch and noticed the back corners of the couch which was being pulled in with thick golden cord tie backs, which I just had to toy with. As I looked down I could see it was standing up from the floor on beautiful ornate ball and claw feet. Then I spotted the pillars at each end of the room, they were standing proud and tall in ivory marble.

"Have you finished playing with my tassels yet?" he asked teasingly.

"Hmm…….?" I mumbled and realised I still had hold of the tie backs "Oh sorry" I replied, laughing at his remark.

Andy was by now observing my reaction to everything and proceeded to guide me over to the en-suite bathroom.

"Come on, have a look in here if you want" he gestured to the en-suite bathroom.

"Oh can I?.......Thanks"

I glanced in through the doorway and saw even more marble tiling on the walls and floor. The white suite was complimenting the room brilliantly, garnished with chrome Italian style taps. Even the towels were ivory and embossed with gold stitching.

"The word palatial springs to mind" I said in an excited tone.

"You're easily pleased, aren't you" he laughed.

"It's just that I'm not used to something this big" I answered and the room certainly did look fabulous and rang true of a grand affair.

"Why don't you sit down and clear your head for a while?" he politely suggested as he strolled off to the bathroom.

"You're right. It is still bothering me"

Whilst Andy disappeared off to the bathroom I tried to clear my mind of any suggestive implications, which could be misconstrued in my presence in a strange man's hotel room. He clearly wanted to make sure that I was being looked after and I knew I had a clear conscience, but I couldn't help feeling a little excitable and tingly, in the prospect of hanging round with a man like him.

Andy joined me on the couch and confirmed his intentions to talk to my boss.

"Right I've had time to think, but I'm a bit too busy tomorrow, so I will be talking to your boss......more than likely the day after tomorrow, if that's okay?" he asked passing my files back to me.

"I'm sure that will be okay" I replied nervously.

"Trust me, after today's meeting I'm fairly certain we'll be able to sort something out" he confirmed.

"You mean regardless of the fact I have managed to embarrass myself....... In the restaurant I mean?"

"Trust me, that one doesn't count............. I did feel worried about you though" he confirmed, graciously refuting the incident. "Believe it or not I have actually managed to block that one from my decision making"

I started to relax and laughed at his amusing response.

"Oh well, that's alright then!"

"Don't worry your contract is still secure. To be honest with you I was quite impressed in your efforts to clinch this one"

The tray of food had just arrived and was being served to us on a small trolley. Andy ushered the waiter to leave and started pouring us some wine, into the two glasses on the tray. On handing me my glass he changed his topic of conversation to a more relaxed introduction into his world. He was logical and decisive in his approach and at the same time he showed a lighter side to him as a way of encouragement, for me to relax. We started to eat our well earned meal. Still chatting away, we managed to devour everything in front of us. First the soup, still piping hot and a supply of seeded, bread rolls.

"Here you are………. your salmon looks nice" he said as he very politely passed me my dinner.

And it was. The salmon in hollandaise sauce and trimmings were cooked to perfection. If I could of got away with licking the plate I would of done. Andy had opted for a more traditional choice.

"I'm sorry, but I can't help thinking if your steak was cooked any less……." I started shocked in seeing how pink it was inside "It's just that it's so rare, it looks like it's going to get up and walk off your plate"

Andy looked across at me for a second and started to laugh at my silly observation and stabbed another piece of steak, dipping it into his black bean sauce.

"Well……..I do like it this way" he confirmed and proceeded to take his next bite.

He seemed to have a really good down to earth attitude. He whittled off his list of typical punters who met with his disapproval. Followed by his moderate sense of humour when it came to the latest text messages. At this he quickly showed me example after example of crude or silly text messages that he had recently received. To which I quickly tried to impress him with my own supply of stimulating text messages, on my mobile phone. Before long we were totally at ease in one another's company, completely relaxed as we slouched back into the couch. Andy had positioned his arm over the back of the couch as he plodded on with his account of various people he came into contact with.

"As I say, this is a blunt reminder to us all" he continued "Their lack of commitment to the job, or just their pathetic miserable excuses for not doing a job."

I just listened offering an occasional smile as he rambled on in a resourceful manner, to which I could relate to quite easily.

"Certain people will reel off their never ending and shallow excuses, when it comes to actually doing a job" he said.

"I know what you mean"

"They only ever care about themselves, do you know what I mean, instead of giving a damn about others?" he asked.

"Definitely, I know someone like that too"

He was so down to earth, so considerate towards the hard workers of this world and at the same time he clearly didn't suffer fools.

He stopped talking for a minute and glanced down at his watch, then back over towards me in a thoughtful yet quizzical way.

"They didn't give us any pills, did they?"

"I'll be alright" I said, knowing fine well that my headache was really bothering me, but not wanting to be rude.

Just then the mobile phone rang out from my handbag. I made my excuses and grabbed the bag and took myself off to the bathroom. James was on the other end checking in.

"Hi James" I said carefully, not wanting to say anything that would give too much of my situation away.

"Hi Tess, how did it go?"

"Oh okay I think, he's reckons I'm in with a chance"

Not wanting to give anything away I opted for a more subtle approach, so I shared with him my version of a hard day's travelling.

"I couldn't figure out the tubes, then I got a massive headache" I said and continued "I think I'll just get my head down"

"You didn't show yourself up then, you remembered to keep quiet?"

"Of course I didn't, any way he's done most of the talking"

"Alright pet listen, I'll let you go and tomorrow I'll cook us something nice for dinner, okay?"

"Sounds good, love you" I answered and he wished me good night in his usually fond way.

It suddenly dawned on me as I closed the phone, that Andy could of overheard me telling someone I was going to go to bed. How would I talk my way out of that one. But as I stepped out of the bathroom I could see Andy, still perched on the couch. I figured he couldn't of heard me, not from that distance, so I felt a sense of relief.

"Do you always take your calls in the bathroom?" Andy quizzed with a pleasant smile on his face.

"Oh sorry. That was James my…." I started, but Andy quickly jumped in.

"I'm joking. Your boyfriend you mean…….come on sit down"

Feeling slightly awkward, I decided to mention James's phone call. I explained my predicament and how embarrassed I had felt cheating James from the truth.

"I couldn't tell him I was in your hotel room, he would never understand" I explained awkwardly.

"I see what you mean" Andy answered and very patiently nodded and agreed this was obviously difficult for me. "Funnily enough, I've just gone through a messy separation . It wasn't a long term relationship or anything, but on reflection I doubt she would of understood either"

"It's just…….I didn't want to be rude in refusing your kind offer of dinner, that's all"

"Listen, I'm sorry if I've put you on the spot" Andy said casually, offering a polite apology for the position he had placed me in.

I sensed a genuine concern in his words as he tried to rectify the situation.

"He does trust you though, doesn't he?"

"Yes!……….. It's more a case of, well………….. he thinks I'm going to say or do something stupid" I started, as Andy listened thoughtfully.

"I assure you, you haven't" he offered, trying to give me some confidence.

"I decided not to mention my fainting expedition in the restaurant" I continued, quickly attempting to change the subject and I started to laugh it off.

"Why?"

Placing my best foot forward I started to walk back to him, then I noticed at the end of the sideboard was a wooden game set of back gammon.

"Do you play?" I quizzed.

"What, backgammon? I haven't played that in years. Bring it over"

Obligingly I picked up the base to the game and carried it across, as if submitting to an order rather than a request. He seemed to have a knack of offering instruction as opposed to suggestions.

"I'm not sure how you position the disc pieces" I continued.

"We'll figure it out…..You were going to tell me why you didn't tell him"

"He always tells me to be careful not to make a fool of myself…..he thinks that I will say or do the wrong thing all the time, that's all"

"That's not very nice. Does he always talk to you like that?" he asked placing a bunch of discs down.

"Usually……."

Before long we had managed to fathom out the correct sequence to positioning the disc pieces and tossed the first dice.

"How long have you been together?" he asked throwing his dice.

"Nearly two years now"

"Two years……..and he's still telling you how to behave?"

"Well yes……why, what do you mean?"

"Well it's none of my business, but I would of thought after that length of time, he would of learned to accept you as you are" he said "Your go!"

"Hmm?" I looked up confused.

"I've played, it's your go" he laughed.

"Oh right......aah that's not fair. I'm going to get you for that" I laughed as Andy managed to remove one of my discs.

And sure enough, on his next throw he had left himself wide open to my next move. He had inadvertently left a disc by itself, rendering it a prisoner on my next throw of the dice.

"Look if you were my girlfriend I'd feel proud of you. Let's face it you're attractive, you've a lovely personality and you can certainly make me laugh" he said flattering me "I'd be proud to have you hanging off my arm!"

"Thanks!" I replied flattered by his comment.

Andy had suddenly placed a seed of doubt into my head and at the same time wrapped it up beautifully with a cherry on top, by concluding his observations with a gracious compliment thrown in.

"Yes!........Got you!" I chanted thoroughly impressed with my stroke of good luck.

He sat back amused by my silly behaviour and chuckled to himself.

"Okay......I will agree to be much more thoughtful, before knocking you off the board again" he said still shaking his head and smiled.

We managed to play a whole game of bullish stubbornness and cunning tricks to knock each other off the board. Laughing as we went, tormenting each other with a toss of the dice, making promises that the next one was definitely going to be a double.

"You know" he continued "Your James can't mould you into what he wants. Look at my last girlfriend. She had to be the most shallow conceited madam, on the face of this earth. It didn't matter how attractive she was I could never of stayed with her"

I couldn't help but nod in agreement, because I knew Andy was actually right.

"So what do you think I should do. I don't mind trying to better myself?"

"That's alright if you want to be like him, I don't have a problem with your level of intelligence, do I?"

"Suppose not" I said mystified, taking his food for thought on board.

And I knew he was right again. One thing that did occur to me was the way we kept in good spirits with each other. It just felt as though we had known each other for years. Here I was in a city hotel, playing backgammon with a top businessman. It was a though we were sat in a country house somewhere. I would have been even more convinced if we had a roaring fire in the background, lying by the hearth and in our pyjamas.

"Look it's like this, look at me for instance" he continued thoughtfully "I didn't leave school with loads of qualifications and I've done alright for myself. You have to be accepted for who you are Tess, don't let him bully you"

"Aah, are you not going to let me have this one?" I teased, trying to make Andy feel bad for nearly knocking me off.

"Oh go on, I'll move this instead" he responded, displaying his gentlemanly skills.

Little did he know that I was really just appealing to his good sense of fair play, whilst fully intending to massacre any hope of him defeating me.

Finally we came to the end of our game and I was convinced Andy had sacrificed himself a few goes earlier, to help me catch up. He still beat me, but only marginally. Sitting back at one with the world, with my head against the back of the couch, my headache reminded me it was still lingering in the background.

"I nearly won" I whispered, fairly satisfied with my attempts to beat him.

"Nearly......better luck next time eh?" he teased, laughing at my comment.

"It's no good. I'm going to have to call it a night"

"To be honest" Andy started "I don't know how you've managed to keep going"

We both slowly walked over to the door to say our goodbyes. I made my way over to the door first and started to offer my appreciation for his hospitality.

"I'd just like to say thank you Andy, for the meal and everything"

"You're welcome Tess Bannister!" he said beaming towards me "I've enjoyed this evening. Actually I've especially enjoyed your company!"

I couldn't help but smile at his friendly comment and stepped to one side as he opened the door for me. He said his goodbyes, shaking my hand and reminded me that he fully intended to get in touch with me at some point in the near future, to try and finish our meeting. I returned back to my room nursing an overtired and weary head and pondered over the next day's daunting task of having to travel back home.

Chapter sixteen

ven though I knew James would be waiting for me I couldn't resist nipping over to Anne's place, to fill her in with the latest gossip. I had just enough time before James would of realised that I had returned. The journey had been fraught with the usual pushing and shoving and backpacks being butted into my shoulder. Nevertheless, I had found myself day dreaming, reliving the previous day's events, while staring out of the carriage window.

Anne was busy wading her way through a well chosen pile of delicates that needed some ironing.

"Go on then" she said encouraging me to spill the beans, while sifting through her ironing.

"It wasn't like meeting a client, at all"

"Well, what was it like?"

"He was different. I mean he was down to earth, like us"

"Was he good looking though?" she enquired optimistically.

"Anne, he was just a client"

"That's why you're here now then isn't it darling. Instead of being with dearest James" she replied, knowing fine well she was right.

I started to tell her all about the idiot in the lift, who'd really got up my nose. Anne started to clap with sheer wickedness at my poor taste in trickery.

"So you actually cheated the poor man out of a tenner, bad girl!" she cheered.

"He wouldn't stop bothering me"

"Yeah. Serves him right then.......Good for you!"

I slowly pieced together each sordid detail. The ridiculous journey, then the lift. The hotel foyer and the embarrassing realisation that my new found client was the same man from the lift. Followed by the inevitable score card, that I couldn't remember filling in. Was he an eight, nine even? I just couldn't decide. I continued on and on, the posh car ride, being driven by the idiot from the lift. I had so much to tell her!

Anne sat and took on board every juicy detail with intrigue, drawing her own conclusions. She just kept watching me, as though what she was really doing was reading my mind.

"I think we'll need a drink for this one"

"Oh, sorry Anne. But I had to tell someone!"

My mind was rushing faster and faster, as I delivered the next detail to my amazing adventure.

"Then I actually fainted in the middle of the restaurant, I mean how embarrassing is that?"

"Oh very" she teased.

"The lack of memory is taunting me" I continued feeling frustrated, as I tried to convince her that my client had actually, not only picked me up, but he had carried me across a crowded restaurant.

"He took care of me, like.......well like a boyfriend would"

"Oh you have been busy" she said toying with me.

"What was that phrase I'd thought up for him, that I promised myself I would share with you?" I said racking my brain.

Anne just sat raising her eyebrows at me, waiting patiently for me to decide.

"Oh yes! I've got it........He was the most suave and sophisticated businessman, ever!"

"Flipping heck, slow down girl" Anne chuckled as she reacted with slight confusion, to my overambitious desire to clamber out the words.

"No, there's more!" I persisted.

"Coffee……..definitely coffee!" she insisted and set off to sort out the drinks.

I followed her into the kitchen, so I could keep going with all the details. I sat and watched her preparing the mugs and tried to mull over in my mind what I wanted to say. Not knowing what I was feeling, all I did know was that I had to clear my head long before facing James.

"James will instantly sense I have a problem just because I'm bursting at the seams"

"No he won't. Look maybe you really need to be asking yourself something else" she started, leading me up to a penultimate question "Maybe darling, you are ready for a change, hmm?"

"No it's not like that…..It's just well…….take the hotel room for example. We played back gammon. I mean…….how did that happen?"

"He treated you like a normal human being that's all" she confirmed.

I wasn't sure what I was thinking but all I knew was, for the first time in absolutely ages, a man had made me feel normal and Anne understood what I was feeling.

"You're right. He didn't make me feel stupid did he? Not even embarrassed even after fainting in front him."

"See, he was just being nice"

"Oh but Anne…..The warmth he showed towards me even though I'd insulted one of his staff."

Anne just laughed and shook her head in frustration. She carried on listening quite intently by this time, as she poured hot water from the kettle into two mugs. She was showing clear signs through her ability to smile throughout, that she had a perfect understanding of my dilemma.

"Thanks" I started as she passed me a mug "I couldn't find Andy at breakfast. I can only presume that he'd already left."

"Well, maybe he had another meeting" she offered, sipping her coffee.

"Do you realise, that final meeting with him didn't happen and I feel as though it had been denied me for some reason" I finished and composed myself as I leaned across her table.

Anne was very good at understanding everything. She had the knack of analysing people very well. Within two minutes of meeting someone, she would have them sussed perfectly . Understanding me came much easier to her simply on the strength of knowing me for so long.

Her friendly answer came very quickly. She wrapped her arms around me from behind and hugged my shoulders.

"You have to calm down sweetie or James will definitely know something's wrong, won't he, eh?"

And I thought 'she's right. After all he was just a client, wasn't he?'. I finally managed to descramble my brain and settled down to the well earned mug of coffee.

"So, what do you think?" I asked.

"It's hard to say really. I mean, it's not as though he's promised you anything, has he?" she said with a reassuring twinkling in her eye.

"No, I suppose not".

At that I carefully re-evaluated the situation. All Andy had really agreed on was, checking in with my boss. If I was to screw this one up now, the chances were I would definitely be looking for a new job. That's torn it. I'd have to accept the fact that all I had really achieved was a new contract. But then I couldn't help remembering his words when he told me he'd especially enjoyed my company.

Anne had set about tackling her chore of doing the ironing, leaving me to quietly contemplate my thoughts. She was good like that, she just took a back seat until I was ready for her to do some more listening. With a deflated impression of myself, I checked my watch for the time and prepared to face James.

"Right, I have to get going" I started and rose to my feet "After all, he's the one cooking dinner for me tonight"

"Are you going to be alright?" she asked as I gathered up my belongings.

"I know you're right, I've just got caught up in the fantasy of everything" I replied, finishing off my coffee.

But I kept thinking that I had actually managed to deviate from the truth, when it came to telling James where I really was last night. I contemplated the question in my head 'How understanding of the situation would I be if the roles had been reversed?'. This one was hard to imagine knowing the way James always showed such control. I hugged Anne and reassured her that I was not going to get too carried away with my emotions. I convinced myself that the important thing to remember was to behave with absolute professionalism, without letting my imagination run away with me.

"You know what I think girl, don't you.........and I'm not saying it's time to move on or anything" she started in reassuring tones "But I think Andy was right, you are too good for James"

"Well James is taking me out to a bankers annual dinner next weekend" I started "So I'll try and talk to him"

"Good luck with that!...............If you haven't read in a paper first though, he won't be listening" she teased.

Anne showed no signs of disapproval towards me, in fact she seemed quite amused by my new lease of energy. I searched my mind for a second or two, for any tell tale signs generating from Anne's normally unforgiving truths and decided it was definitely time to head off back to James's house.

"Bye darling, take care and tell me everything" Anne concluded, offering me another hug.

"Bye Anne.....and thanks"

We arranged a rendezvous for our usual lunchtime banter and I kissed her farewell at the door. With my mind sufficiently cleared of any misdemeanours and silly intentions, I knew that I could face James with honesty in my heart and no reprisals to fall my way.

As I headed off towards James's house I started to think about the other important things in life, such as dressing up for yet another special occasion. With Christmas looming ever nearer and all the festivities to look forward to, did I really want to rock the boat over a misunderstood trip to London? I battled on a while longer to try to reassure myself with answers to my reckless thoughts. I felt myself beginning to smile at my foolishness and decided no harm had been done and my reputation was still in tact.

Chapter seventeen

I t wasn't so much the day of reckoning as much as the night of reckoning. The Bankers Christmas Dinner was finally upon us again and I was thinking it wasn't going to be the most exciting box that I'd ticked on my calendar this year. Most evenings like this usually proved to be rather slow to start, dull in the middle and generally ending with a disappointing thud at the end. Some miracle of miracles may have decided to take charge of the situation and render us with more a upbeat and chatty crowd this time, instead of the usual two left footed brigade for company.

James in his wisdom had agreed for us to meet up with his bank manager and other guests at a local hotel. Inside there was the tallest Christmas tree, a good 10 foot in height, being displayed in the main hall. We stopped over at the table plan which had been carefully situated on a tall standing easel and checked for our names.

Fortunately it wasn't a black tie do so James had stuck to a more traditional suit and tie, whilst I had invented a new look from my tired wardrobe. After receiving our first complimentary glass of white wine we sought out the appropriate faces that only James could identify. I swiftly jumped into action as any good and proper girlfriend would do and started to use my usual charming greeting skills on the guests.

"Oh hi, hi.......yes hi" I greeted enthusiastically.

This I have to say is normally appreciated by most of the men, but as a general rule this is usually disapproved of by the ladies, especially when I took too long about it.

"Good evening" came a disgruntled reply from a stern faced woman, maybe this was because I'd just finished planting a generous kiss on her husband's cheek.

I never mean to offend the other women in the room it's just that I have an absolute craving for attention and I'm driven with so much adrenalin, I always manage to rub them up the wrong way.

"Oh don't worry........your husband's quite safe" I said.

"Tess" warned James, slightly worried by the woman's reaction.

"Oh James I just sometimes, you know.... I just get carried away with the hugging and kissing"

"Well she's obviously not amused is she?" he chastised, crossly.

"But I'm just being polite" I pleaded feeling a little deflated.

Do I really want to apologise for being funnier or more attractive than some of them. Maybe I should become more conservative with my dress sense or even learn to talk in that particularly sweet tone? Or maybe not. It just wasn't me! That is an utterly sickly idea and left me feeling like I'd just stepped down the aisle of a church, in my floral pinny with great grandmamma.

As we prepared to take our places at the table I couldn't help but notice the bankers in their dull, boring suits, sat round the table partnering their cardboard cut out wives with vacant expressions slapped across their faces. No talent spotting or stimulating conversations were going to arise from this table tonight. As I looked around and smiled at the unfamiliar faces, James saw fit to lean across and suggested something very politely into my ear.

"If you sit there quietly, say nothing and just observe what's going on you may just learn something" he whispered.

"Ooh, let's think about that for a minute" I mused "Yes! I'm convinced, it works for me!"

James showed me a tell tale look, that suggested he was less than pleased with my witty remark. Apparently it was a sign of intelligence to just listen and smile because it gave the illusion that I knew more than I was letting on. Well on that basis I had nothing to lose then, after all it had been suggested on previous occasions, the one thing I can't do is switch my brain on into the right gear.

As I peered across the tables I could see the typical displays of party poppers, crackers and party hats lying dormant on the tables, evidence that Christmas was here again. The traditional turkey dinner and stuffing was about to be served. I couldn't help wishing my friends were here to help spur me on.

"Are you alright Tess?" James asked.

"I don't really know anyone" I replied, feeling a little bored.

"Don't worry, I only know Michael"

"Who's Michael?"

"Oh Tess, do you ever listen?.......he's our bank manager for the office" he said smiling at my confusion.

"Oh.......well, I'm just bored of not having anyone to talk to"

"Listen it'll be dancing soon. Just wait"

So I waited as patiently as was humanly possible. I couldn't help but notice that on the table next to ours was a woman showing more cleavage than was completely necessary. Nevertheless, she was showing signs that she had made much more of an effort, in her particularly stunning sequined gown than everyone else on her table. Her partner next to her was busy laughing and displaying the best set of whitened teeth I'd seen in ages. Disappointed in the fact that we hadn't sat at their table and enjoying ourselves in their company, I settled my thoughts on arousing James leg under the table. Not immune to my obvious choice of affections James instinctively obliged me with one of his endearing smiles and caressed the top of my hand with his. We often sent signals to each other from beneath the table, just to let each other know we were still there. Every now and again James decided to bring me into the conversation.

"Didn't we love?"

"Yes" I replied, not hearing a word he'd just spoken.

Our dinner plates had been removed by this time and I watched with keen interest as the waitresses started to arrive with a choice of Christmas pudding or trifle.

"We did, didn't we Tess?" James chirped up in order for me to be accepted into the discussion.

"Oh sorry, yes we did" I acknowledged trying to save my embarrassment, as I was clearly losing the plot.

I made my excuses to go to the ladies and hit the latest imaginary catwalk with a steady pace and proceeded to the waiting queue.

James took it upon himself to do a bit of his own wandering and spied an old face. He made his way over to the table next to ours.

"Hey James, good man!" the man greeted.

"You alright, Steve, how are you doing?"

"Not so bad......have you heard, I've moved to the London branch now"

"Side tracked or promoted?" James teased.

"Eh, watch it.......promoted of course" replied Steve, laughing at James's banter.

"Hi, how are you?" James asked of Steve's wife.

"Oh sorry mate, this is Janet my wife" Steve quickly offered as Janet held out her hand to shake with James, still grinning at her husband.

"I wondered when you were going to say something love" she started "Where's your wife gone?"

"Oh she's not my wife, that's just my girlfriend Tess" James offered "She's just gone to the powder room"

"She's looking really well James, so when will you be popping the question then, eh?" teased Steve encouragingly.

"Yeah right"

"We'll come and say hello later, okay" said Janet and turned to finish off her pudding.

On my return I noticed James had started up a conversation with the man with very white teeth. He saw me coming back and quickly resumed his place as I sat back down. He just smiled and patted my knee as we finished off our cups of coffee and complimentary mints. At this stage it was James's turn to get up and leave the table.

I observed the guests at our table for a few minutes and looked on as they started to disburse and soon I found myself alone. Pulling my chair out to stretch my legs I repositioned and sat back down.

Before long James and the couple from the next table came over to join me. James was by this time standing alongside me, as he started introducing Steve and his wife to me.

"This is Janet"

"Hi Janet, I love your dress" I offered.

"Hi I'm Steve. You look lovely tonight sweetheart" Steve said beaming at me.

"Thanks, haven't we met before?" I enquired, convinced I would of remembered that set of teeth anywhere.

"Last year, but I was over at the Manchester branch then. I've been at London's head office since then" Steve responded, keen to share his promotion with us.

It turned out Steve Holt was from Manchester and earned himself quite a high position up the promotional ladder. He and his wife had apparently been invited to join in by one of his branch managers.

The miracle I had been hoping for was stood in front of me, smiling away and shaking my hand. Janet promptly sat down in front of me. She decided to give me the full account of her two children, who incidentally went to the best Grammar school around. And even though when it came to discussions relating to children, I would feel like I was losing the will to live; I listened to what was to become quite a funny story. I found myself laughing along to her humorous banter and couldn't help thinking that she would fit in with my friends really well. And then came the laugh.

"I don't tell him anything.......he just finds out when he gets the bank statement!" said Janet and let out a rip roaring laugh.

"Oh you'd get on with Anne" I shared "She's got a laugh just like that"

"Well you can't keep it in, can you?" she replied and laughed even more.

Janet had to be the jolliest person in the whole room with the exception of her husband.

"Anyway, when is James going to make a good woman out of you?" she quizzed.

"Oh, nothing's been decided really"

"Well I haven't been to a good wedding in ages" she continued and turned to her husband "Steve, when was the last time we went to a wedding?"

"I can't remember, why.......is someone getting married" Steve replied, offering me a teasing wink.

I couldn't work out if James had said anything to them or it was just an innocent question, but I was careful not to catch a glimpse of James's face. I didn't want to spoil anything.

Knowing that James was standing alongside me, I continued to listen to Janet's long list of repartee and decided to arouse James with my affections once more. I started to pinch his waist, then tugging at his waistband as I slipped my hand in through the inside of his jacket and promptly offered a gentle squeezing pinch to his bottom. I continued to reassure Janet that I was still paying attention with quick gestures.

"Oh, did he?" I said

"But obviously I was the last one to know anything"

"Really, well I didn't know either. James doesn't tell me anything"

"Men I ask you, what are they like?" said Janet and continued to laugh again.

At the same time I busied myself by squeezing my fingers in through James's cuff and up inside his sleeve. I gently pulled at the hairs on his wrist and massaged his arm up and down with my fingertips. He seemed to respond very calmly as he stood quietly by my side.

All of a sudden Janet looked behind her and turned back to face me, grinning; then she started to giggle. Then the realisation kicked in. Coming towards me was James, who had apparently swapped places with Steve at some point without me even noticing. Whilst I had been listening to Janet, it was she who had monitored the swap over and found herself amused by the incident. Fortunately, she had realised the intended victim was meant to be James.

"What is it?" asked James, somewhat puzzled by all the grinning faces.

"Your better half has........well let's just say, she's been very entertaining" Steve replied thoroughly amused by the whole thing.

As James took a careful glance over at me, looking obviously confused, Steve started to explain to him what had just been going on. He vividly explained away in a somewhat exaggerated and dramatically demonstrated replay, re-enacting my moves.

"You really shouldn't of stopped you know. I was enjoying that!" he chuckled.

"Yes, alright......it wasn't that funny, really" I said indignantly.

"Oh sorry Steve......Tess has had too much to drink, again" said James.

In my embarrassment I looked up towards James, expecting him to chastise me. As the couple continued to laugh James simply grinned with amusement and realised the mix up. He pleasantly smiled down at my somewhat red face.

"Never mind pet, maybe you can show me later"

Steve smiled and walked away from us for a moment. Janet was busy chatting to some other people, filling them in with the details of my mix up. Steve suddenly returned with an unexpected surprise and handed me a well chosen bouquet of flowers, which had been left in the middle of his table as a centre piece.

"Here you are love. I think you've earned these" he teased, handing them over to me

and with that we all started to laugh again.

The slow dances had started and we all wandered on to the dance floor. James wrapped his arm around my back and pulled me in, slowly stroking my hair and offered a caressing tweak to my chin.

"Don't worry, it's only Steve.....he will have forgotten by tomorrow" he tried to reassure me.

"Sorry, but I really did think it was you!" I replied, but I couldn't help thinking that this was not going to be the end of the matter.

As we danced I kept thinking that knowing my luck every fax machine and email sent out from Steve's bank was going to link back to my personal embarrassment.

"Flattered or not, I can't see him dropping this one in a hurry" I whispered, but James just pulled me in further dancing out the last dance, drawing the evening's entertainment to a close.

Chapter eighteen

Just across the way from Stacey's work was a small but friendly coffee house. For the first time in ages our usual haunt for lunch was too busy. So here we were trying out a new venue, so we could play catch up on the latest gossip.

As I waited for my chicken salad pancetta, I started to bring the girls up to speed on James's latest choice of outings.

"You'll never guess where James is taking me now" I said while sipping on my cappuccino.

"Go on then……… If you must" retorted Stacey.

"A school reunion!"

"Don't you mean an old toffs seminar!" chanted Anne clearly amusing herself.

"Well, I can top that one. I'm going to see Mark's parents this weekend" said Stacey with obvious disapproval; introducing us into the world of her never ending new boyfriends.

"Even worse!" I giggled "So who's Mark when he's at home?" I asked curiously trying to coax her into divulging her latest secret.

"What is it about men eh? They can't help themselves can they?" Continued Anne as she carried on scoffing on her cheesy baguette "I mean they have to just bore the pants off us and then we are expected to be grateful or something"

"Oh that's right! Have you got out of going to see Richard's family this Christmas yet, or are you still working out an excuse for that one?" I teased.

"Yeah, you can mock. Who will you be dating this Christmas then?" Anne taunted with evil intent.

"Hmm excuse me, does anybody even want to know?" Stacey asked disappointed in our lack of enthusiasm.

Anne and I just looked at each other and pretended to not be interested. I winked at Anne, knowing that Stacey would be oblivious to our deliberate teasing, whilst Anne pretended to be deaf.

"I read somewhere..." I said.

"What was that James? Honestly, I mean you even sound like him now" scoffed Stacey obviously unimpressed with me. I couldn't help but be amused and gently chuckled through my nose.

"Perhaps I should keep quiet about James"

"I've recited a whole list of ideas for Richard. So now he knows exactly what he has to buy me for Christmas this year" continued Anne, pushing Stacey further out of the conversation.

It never ceased to amaze me how she could manage to manipulate a man into buying her so much stuff. Her lack of conscience as she paraded her partner's eyes across the latest in expensive cleansers, to dragging him across town to the jewellers new no bounds.

"Amazingly........" continued Anne still finishing a bite of her lunch " he always insists on buying me the things that I've always wanted. He's got great taste in presents!" Anne smirked in satisfaction at her own matter of fact statement.

"Yeah right. What a coincidence............... I don't think!" I replied sniggering.

But by now Stacey was bursting at the seams to pour out her wonderful news about her latest boyfriend.

"Mark definitely has to be the perfect man!" she said desperately trying to be heard.

"Well, all I can say Stacey darling………" started Anne smugly "Those tell tale signs you seem to be giving away, can only mean one thing. Right Tess?"

"Oh definitely!"

"What?" and by now Stacey was becoming thoroughly frustrated with our silliness.

"Well she has to be………. You know, definitely getting enough this month. Right Tess?" tormented Anne.

I couldn't help laughing at Anne's wicked sense of humour. But tried to discreetly put poor Stacey out of her misery.

"You are blossoming girl……the tell tale signs are all too abundantly clear" I confirmed still smiling at her radiating enthusiasm.

Stacey started to blush and resigned herself to the fact that her friends were not only right, but all too aware that she had started to enjoy herself again in the men's department. Anne and I also knew that we could not argue with Stacey's taste in men, seeing as she hadn't allowed Mark his coming out session with us yet. Unable to vet this man left us in no doubt, that if he was 'mister right' we would of met him by now. Nevertheless, the fact that he was helping her to blossom again was good enough for us.

At the end of all our gossiping we did our usual hugging and waved each other off. Just in time for me to return to my designated work place, to resume my underpaid and under appreciated role to finish off the afternoon.

Whilst I was busy racing off back to work, the girls stayed behind to finish their coffees.

"What's wrong with Tess" asked Stacey as she finished off her coffee.

"Isn't it obvious, London……Work it out girl?" replied Anne sniggering slyly into her latte.

"I don't get it…….."

"Put it this way……..Tess has been treated to a new lease of life with you know who" replied Anne, hinting towards Andy Carter.

"She didn't……………. did she?" asked Stacey startled by the new revelation.

"No......but I bet, given half the chance she would have liked to" Anne teased nodding in confirmation towards Stacey.

"Is she going to see him again then... do you think?" continued Stacey with curios tones built into her question.

"Oh, I think he's definitely given her food for thought. Put it this way Stacey, she couldn't face James afterwards. What does that tell you, eh?"

"Oooh naughty girl. Mind you, it would serve James right after the way he's been treating her lately"

"Watch this space darling......watch this space!" said Anne with delicious intent in her voice.

Chapter nineteen

The next few days seemed to go very fast. All of the Christmas and New Year celebrations were upon us and it was as though the never ending spending that you have to do at this time of year had made it compulsory to stay indoors. My vane hope was to rescue the old bank balance from dying on me completely, so I made a huge effort to be good with my spending.

My boss had already informed me that Mr Carter had signed a five year contract with the firm so my bonus for the month was secure, but it still meant I had to be a little bit thrifty with my spending habits.

I had taken the afternoon off as James was escorting me to an old boy's reunion. The phone was ringing back at the office and I had asked Amy to take my calls.

"Hello Amy speaking, how may I help you?" she sang rather eloquently down the telephone.

"Hi, can I speak to Tess Bannister please?"

"Oh I'm sorry sir. She's out of the office for the rest of the day. Can I help?" and the caller thought for a moment unsure of his next move.

"Actually, it really is Tess that I need to speak to. I don't suppose you could tell me her mobile number could you?"

"Oh sorry, I'm not at liberty to give that information out sir. What is it regarding?" Amy persisted.

The caller felt a little disillusioned at the lack of assistance he was getting, but decided to persevere. "Listen, I understand the position I'm placing you in, but you see I just need to keep an appointment with her. It is important"

"I don't usually……..wait, hang on a minute" Amy started, trying to find a solution to the problem "I could give you her e-mail address. Would that help?"

"Brilliant, let me get a pen" he replied satisfied with Amy's answer and proceeded to take the details.

James drove up the gravel drive heading towards a most impressive, charming and antiquated building. I felt a tingling sensation pass through me. There was ivy climbing the walls as far as the eye could see, making an opening for the huge wooden doors. I couldn't help noticing the really old chimney stacks protruding from the roof tops and rows upon rows of windows lining the length and breadth of the old bricked walls.

"You went to school here?" I asked shocked in the immenseness of the place.

"What did you expect Tess?" he laughed pleased with my enthusiasm.

There was a typical display of pretentious cars lining the driveway and entrance and James pulled in alongside them.

"Come on Tess, don't fidget like that"

"I'm not fidgeting. I'm just straightening my outfit"

"We can go this way" he said as he guided me in through the main entrance.

James sauntered two steps ahead of me, checking out all the old plaques decorating the walls. Then he crossed over to some old wooden cabinets and peered through the glass displays.

"That was our class" he said pointing his finger occasionally and reminiscing over passed memories.

"Fascinating!"

James offered me a sharp eye of disapproval and persisted in entertaining me with even more of his drivel. From there he quickly drew me over to some elongated pictures, dragging the length of the corridor, with scenes of old sports teams and years old class photo shoots. Try as I might I could not bring myself to get into the swing of things.

Typically, just at the crucial point of James's historical account my phone started to ring. I quickly reached into my bag to retrieve the offending noise and turned to see a grimace on James's face.

"I won't be long. You go on ahead" I said and proceeded to take the call. "Hello"

"Hi Tess, its Amy"

"What's up Amy? You knew I wasn't coming in this afternoon"

"Sorry Tess, but I've just had a really weird phone call from some guy, asking for you. He wanted to speak to you so I told him you were out. Then he said he wanted your number. Odd I thought 'cause I didn't recognise his voice. Well I didn't think you'd want me to just give it out. What do you think?"

"No, I suppose not. Did he give his name?"

"Oh sorry, I didn't think to ask him. But it doesn't matter anyway 'cause I gave him your email address instead. You can give him your number yourself then can't you?"

"I suppose so. Thanks Amy. See you later. Bye"

At that I quickly caught up with James and resumed my place by his side.

"Sorry James. I'll switch it off, okay?"

James seemed completely oblivious to my absence, but after a few minutes he turned to me and gave me a thoughtful smile. He started to gently influence me with his thoughts of wisdom.

"The importance of conducting oneself is crucial at a time like this. You will remember that, won't you Tess?"

And there it was. It had become abundantly clear that his image was more important to James than showing off his well dressed girlfriend.

"Eeh well, I ....I'll have to think about that then won't I?" I uttered in the most ridiculous common accent I could muster.

"Tess!"

"Just kidding, where's you're sense of humour gone?"

"Not now Tess please, okay?" he persisted "Just behave with a little more decorum"

We arrived in the centre of the school grounds which appeared to be an old square courtyard. Some charming young boys stood back and waited to offer us a complimentary glass of wine from their outstretched trays. As we sipped our drinks we ventured across the old cobbled slabs to join up with some of his old colleagues. The pathway in front left me in the belief that we had stepped back in time. I looked on as the men started to mingle and voiced their strong beliefs on each other in authoritative tones. Then their systematic rituals of random handshakes began. Their high pitched voices rang out as they acknowledged an old friend's arrival. James by now was in hot pursuit of some old friends in the furthest corner, with me trailing behind him reluctantly.

Listening in on one of James's charming conversations that was keeping his audience entertained, I stood poised and waited patiently for the expectant introduction to his discussion. Before long it became apparent that James was going to need some gentle persuasion in allowing me to join in on his talks. After all I had heard it all before and was party to the events that he was discussing anyway. I listened some more and I mused occasionally nodding in agreement to show my interest. Smiling up at James whilst he gave his accurate account of a situation that had taken place, I took it upon myself to join in.

"He could have knocked me for five when he told me that" I interrupted eagerly.

"Six sweetheart. I think you meant to say *six* not five" One of the men replied chuckling.

And with that I slowly retreated, still smiling yet slightly confused and strolled over to the refreshments laid out in front of me. Uncertain of quite what it was that I had just said, that had so obviously amused the man so much, I couldn't help but hear the remnants of a giggle behind me.

One or two of the ladies had begun to join the refreshment stand.

"Hello" one lady said and promptly leaned over the table to pick at some nibbles.

"Hi" I replied politely and casually admired the delicious options of cream cakes, thinly cut sandwiches and nibbles.

"Did I just see you with James?"

"Aha, we've just arrived."

"I hear he's a big shot solicitor now" she said, still picking at the offerings of food laid out.

The assorted bite sized portions of rolled up ham, filled with cheese and chives spread wetted my appetite so I started to fill my plate.

"Hi dear, how are your children doing" came another voice alongside me.

"Me oh sorry, I don't........" I started.

"No dear, I was talking to Melissa.......how's Alistair doing?" a second woman interrupted.

I suddenly sensed that I had just had my nose put out of joint and decided it was time to step aside for the women to do their ritual gossiping. I stood back and observed as a woman next to us attempted to impress us all with her talent in carving a thick slab of scone, topped with layers of jam and cream, with a fork.

"Sorry dear, I didn't mean to be rude" said the second woman insisting on talking to me.

"Oh don't worry..........Why she can't just shove it in her mouth and darn a perfectly orderly moustache of cream pulp like the rest of us could, I don't know" I replied amused by the woman's eating habits.

"That's Peter's wife. She's got two children and she always pigs out at these events"

answered the second woman, laughing at my silly remark.

"There's always been staggering evidence that if you choose the wrong thing to eat, there is every possibility, no probability that you are going to end up dribbling something down the front of your new blouse" I continued, showing my obvious warped sense of humour was still in tact.

Finishing my snack I decided to collect just one more glass of wine from the stand and feeling a little bored with the proceedings returned to where James was standing, still discussing something with keen enthusiasm and amusement. As I moved in on the group of cheerful men I sensed that all was not well. And I was right. To my shock I could hear the faint yet distinct overtones of James's voice in sarcastic banter.

"Typical member of the fairer sex, she's intellectually challenged when it comes to general knowledge you know...." James quipped obviously unaware that I was just behind him.

"Pretty little thing though isn't she?" I heard one of them say with his back to me.

"She's the walking talking proof that for intelligent people like us, bimbo's like her should only ever be seen and never heard" And with that James carried on contorting his face and pointing his finger towards his brain in a silly fashion.

Then it came to me, the realisation of knowing this was one of his worst digs of all time. There it was the final nail in his long overdue coffin. The humiliation of hearing his words and the utter indignation I was feeling as he excused my foolishness to his old school chums in that demoralising way. In his eagerness to impress them James had seen fit to redeem himself with total disregard for my feelings and had failed to notice me, standing within hearing range just behind him. It wasn't as much the feeling of becoming as sober as a judge extremely quickly; as much as wanting to wake up the dead and to send them across to hit him over the back of his miserable head with their spinal cords.

"Are you trying to tell them I'm as thick as two short planks?" I bellowed and true of all good movies, I sensed the volume of noise and chattering had been reduced to hearing a pin drop

Everyone had stopped talking and proceeded to engage their attentions towards us. Oh god; I had finally managed to top James's humiliating one liners with an even more stupid claim of my own, in front of all his privately well-educated old school toffs.

I stopped for a second and composed myself in order to reflect on my next move. If I was to escape this nightmare with any dignity at all, I knew I had to come up with a cunning plan. Unscrambling the jigsaw pieces of the well worn 'must use column' in my head, I decided now was the time to come up with something which would pack such a punch, these men would have to take me seriously once and for all, especially James.

And with that in mind I sauntered over to where they stood and interrupted them, with a disgruntled tapping on James's shoulder for him to turn and face me. At the same time, he was still trying to offer his apologies on my behalf to his amused onlookers. I composed myself for the inevitable challenge of all. There was a constant reminder of unforgiving tears filling my eyes, I wiped away the sprays of dampened makeup upon my cheeks, cleared my throat and in a flash it came to me, 'I've got it!'

I braised myself and cleared my throat for the longest insult to be hurled from my lips, that I could muster.

"Here are some of my salient points of contention, James!" I started and in raised tones I continued on as best I could.

"On one hand it's clear to me that you are an absorbent minefield of information. Yet on the other hand you are still nothing more than a Jumped up, pompous asshole!

No matter how much I try to please you, you still reward me with more of your insults. Just because you may think it's crucial to conduct oneself in a certain way, I don't. I think it's much more important to like myself first, middle and last, rather than be like you! Besides you're nothing more than a sanctimonious prick and ultimately you have played your last card in the pack .... the joker!"

I swallowed hard, knowing my tears were betraying me in full force, but decided to carry on attacking him with just one more insult.

"I have news for you James .... You are the joke. Not me!"

Phew, I actually managed to pour out the words in a stream of precise and accurate sentences. James, still utterly confused by my reprisals looked helpless as he twitched and fidgeted in sheer desperation to fix the problem, much to the amusement of his long lost mates. Feeling thoroughly chuffed with myself I about turned and headed across the courtyard, being careful not to look back at the staggered expressions on their faces. I sped out through the old school doors and off to a comfortable safe zone to collect my thoughts.

Chapter twenty

Slamming the front door to my apartment behind me and flicking the lock firmly on the latch, I had finally made it home. After traipsing through the endless streets of an unknown town I had managed to take a bus ride back to my own familiar ground, still mopping my tears of anguish. Instinctively I decided to start washing James out of my life for good. So I threw down my bag and phone over the back of my settee, then set off to the bathroom to hit the shower.

After washing out the remains of my streaky, rasher stained face in the shower I proceeded to fit into my comfy dressing gown and slippers and gathered up my mop of wet hair into a warmed towel and looked into the mirror. Gazing back at me was the un-tantalising signs of missed mascara smudging the contours of my eyes. With cotton balls and creams at the ready I cleaned up the image looking back from the mirror.

The day from hell was nearly over and no matter how I looked at it, this time there was to be no turning back for me. I knew that finally James and I were officially over. If I could think of an answer to undo all those stupid and foolish things I've ever done over the years, after today's performance, I would well and truly hide it in the recycling bin and forget about it.

I couldn't help but thinking that long miserable days like this had to be shut out, behind closed curtains, as if in a mental state of denial by removing any evidence that the rest of the world truly exists. So I slowly closed the curtains, slumped my way round across the sitting room floor and set about lighting my array of scented candles by the tele. I poured myself a lonely glass of wine and placed it down on the floor next to the candles. Lying on the settee were the tell tale signs that James was still trying to get through to me. The mobile phone, now firmly set on silent, was flashing his name up at me and I quickly pretended not to notice. But for some reason I decided pick up the phone, as if to squeeze the life out of it and instantly threw it back down. I turned away for a moment and then out of sheer frustration I doubled over with the pain of the ridicule I had just endured. Holding on to my stomach, as the reality started to kick in, I decided to talk to James. Well not really talk to James as much as to the mobile phone itself. Safe in the knowledge that the phone couldn't hurt me back.

I reached down and started to bring the phone up to my face, then in the most condescending of tones I could muster; I raised my voice and shouted at the screen in front of me.

"Seven times you've tried to phone James. Seven…well it serves you right!"

I thought to myself 'this feels good' and with a final push I continued on.

"This time, let's see how you like being seen and not heard!" And with this I hurled the phone back into one of the cushions and walked away.

My journal note to myself for today had to be thought out and savoured over a nice glass of wine. So as I reached down for my glass and opened my diary to today's date, I took up my pen to do some serious writing. Opening up the laptop on the floor by my feet, to see the latest daily ritual of e-mails, I slumped down on my back and contemplated the lines in the chapter of my never ending saga. I considered my options and tossing them over in my blissfully drunk head I recited, with a slightly snobbish deliverance.

"Love is crap! Yes really crap!"

I immediately turned over on to my front and leaned towards my diary, I started to write it down. Then followed by:

Love is: to hate all members of the male species' and then scribbled it out quickly, knowing fine well I didn't really mean it. Thoroughly fed up I took another swig from my glass and read it back to myself. 'For goodness sake, get a grip of yourself' I thought and promptly scribbled out the line.

Finally after some deliberations over a few more much needed sips of wine, I started to write again:

'Love is: knowing when to bin all those toffee nosed w*nck*rs and remember to love yourself first!' and started to let the tears of hurt reappear on my face, feeling thoroughly miserable.

From the corner of my eye I spotted the email sign flashing in the corner of my laptop screen. I thought for a moment 'if that's James, he is so going to get a rude awakening from me!'.

But as the page came up on the screen I looked on in disbelief. To my surprise it wasn't a message from James at all. There in front of my eyes lay the most refreshing and quite exciting clue to the contents of this particular email I could of ever read.

'ANYONE FOR BACKGAMMON!!!'

Immediately I set about reading the email and sure enough it was from Andrew Carter, who had obviously returned from London. Apparently he couldn't get hold of me, so I read on:

Sorry I couldn't stay, but would you like to try again; would you be interested in a meal and if so, I will be in Cheshire, in two weeks time.

Considering the fact that I had rendered myself incapable on the first attempt to have a meal with him, how on earth could I possibly refuse him. After all Cheshire was nothing more than an hour's drive from here. And there it was. The answer to my journal. Topping up my empty glass whilst reminiscing over my last stay in London, I sat back to write my next thoughtful piece for the day *'Love is: to always end your day on a high note'.*

As I stared into the tall mirror over my overfilled glass of wine, I pulled down the robe from my shoulder and turned round to take a look at my side view. I took a cheeky look back at my reflection, offering it a teasing pose. As I twisted and turned, admiring the sensual contours of my towelling robe, I reminded myself I've still got what it takes and blew myself a well earned kiss. Then I smiled back at the reflection, taking my last sip of wine for the day.